The Benjamenta College *of* Art

Alan Reed

The Benjamenta College *of* Art

PEDLAR PRESS

ST. JOHN'S

For information, write Pedlar Press at
113 Bond Street, St. John's NL A1C 1T6 Canada

Cover Art	Benjamin Sack, *Metropolis Study*, 2017
Proofreading	Ken Sparling
Design	Emma Dawn Allain
Typeface	Arno Pro
Printed in Canada	Coach House Printing, Toronto

Library and Archives Canada Cataloguing in Publication

Title: The Benjamenta College of Art / Alan Reed.

Names: Reed, Alan, 1978- author.

Identifiers: Canadiana 20190196068 | ISBN 9781989424018 (softcover)

Classification: LCC PS8635.E35 B46 2020 | DDC C813/.6—dc23

Acknowledgements

The publisher wishes to thank the Canada Council for the Arts and the NL Publishers Assistance Program for their generous support of our publishing program.

Nothing
Will have taken place
But the place

—STÉPHANE MALLARMÉ

Prologue

*H*ere is a street. It is a narrow street and it is an old street, it is a street that winds and turns and as it winds and turns it knots itself up with other streets, because it is not the only street here, there are others, there are no end of others, and all of these streets knot themselves up and lie tangled together. They are touching but not quite, and in the gaps between them are buildings, and the buildings are piled one on top of another wherever there is room for one, and even where there is not there is somehow a way to fit another one in anyway, and all together these buildings and streets and the buildings and streets just beyond them, and the ones just beyond those, all of this is a city.

Here is a boy walking down this street, this particular street. Buildings crowd up close to him on one side and close on the other; they are so close that the street is only a trickle running between them and he walks down it, he turns at a corner and here is another narrow and winding street, and this other street is the kind of street that should have shops along it and so there are shops all along it—here is a shop selling toys and here is a shop with a tailor sitting in the window, mending a pair of trousers, here is a shop selling sweets and next door to it a shop selling bitters. They are tiny shops bunched up too close together, one beside the other all up and down the street, and in every one of them the shelves are packed full of whatever it is that particular shop sells. Even the windows are taken over by potted petunias or a rack of light cotton dresses all in a row, or a shelf of mystery stories or penny romances, he cannot quite tell which, or guides to the cultivation of mushrooms, and sometimes in some of the shops there is too much stuff and not nearly enough room for everything that has to fit inside. When this happens—and it happens quite often, especially when the weather is nice—the shops spill out into the street and here and there among the crates and the tables set out on the sidewalk are shopkeepers settled in comfortably among whatever it is they happen to be selling. They sit in folding chairs or they stand with an elbow propped on a window ledge, and while they wait for someone to stop and buy a windup toy or a basket of peaches they watch with nearly interested eyes as the street carries on its way past them.

It is late on a summer afternoon and it is a late summer afternoon, the sky is clear and there is a slight breeze stirring at the edges of things and here is a shop selling flowers, another selling spices and preserves, another with produce stacked in crates on the sidewalk in front of it. The shopfronts blur one into another as the boy walks past and now and then a street light pokes up from the ground in front of one of them, like an improbable sort of tree. Here is another shop selling whatever it sells, sometimes it is hard to tell from just glancing in the window while walking past, and then another, he walks past it too and after these two are more shops and then there is not. Where there should be a shop there is not anything at all, there is a gap in the street and on the other side of it is another shop and another after it and so on, but here there is not, here there is not anything at all and a gate propped up in front of it. It is an iron gate, it should be a solid gate but it is altogether too old to be anything like solid and instead it is a crooked and rickety gate that does not close properly anymore, no matter how firmly it is shut it always swings slightly open again and the boy stops here, in front of this gate. His name is Luca, his hair is almost long, almost but not quite, it has not quite tipped over into being long and it is just shaggy instead. He did not want to be bothered by it, he did not want to always be going in to have his hair cut and so he stopped, and his hair has grown and then grown some more and now it is another sort of problem, bits of it are always floating up from his head and trailing around his ears and getting into his eyes, while he was walking a bit of it drifted down to tickle at his nose and he had to raise a hand to brush it away, but he is getting used to all of that. He is not from here, he has come here from somewhere far away and he must find a particular gate on a particular street somewhere in this city he does not know, and there is more to it than that but for now it is enough to say that he is looking for a gate on a particular street, and this is the street and what if this is the gate.

He bites his lip, because this could be the gate; he reaches out a hand to touch it without being sure if it actually is this gate, if he should touch it or if he should not, and he touches it anyway without having figured it out one way or the other and when he does it moves slightly. It might not mean anything that it does, it might only be that it does not close properly anymore, but Luca decides that it does mean something, that it is an invitation of some sort, he leans into it and it creaks and slowly it opens and beyond it is a lane. The walls of the shops to either side of the lane slump up against it and beyond them are other kinds of buildings, some may be shops but others are not, Luca cannot tell what they are other than that they are not shops, and they are huddled so close together that he does not think there could possibly be enough room between them for the lane to wind through on its way to whatever is at the other end of it, and yet it does. He goes through the gate and tries to close it behind him, and of course it will not close all the way but he closes it as far as it will go, and once he turns away it will creak slightly open again. On this side of the gate there are cobblestones under his feet, they are old and worn smooth and some are cracked down the middle and in the cracks and the gaps between them small shoots of green sometimes reach up from the ground beneath, and the buildings around him all stand still, like trees in an old, old forest, and a hush spreads from them, as if to mark a solemn occasion of some sort or another. Luca steps into the lane and in and out of the shadows cast by the buildings to either side of him, sometimes a little bit of light slips past them but mostly there are buildings between him and the sun, and in the shadows it is not warm like a summer day should be, there is a mustiness to the air instead, like the smell of earth, and somehow he cannot hear the city that is only a few steps away, somehow it is quiet here. Sometimes he walks past a window set deep into a wall, one that looks in on a room that is not meant to be looked in on; in them he sees shelves laden with forgotten boxes and dust lying thick on them, or with sheets draped over them to protect them from the dust, and once he sees someone wearing overalls and leaning wearily on a mop in the space between two rows of shelves. Luca catches only a glimpse of whoever it is but he does not stop for a better look, he keeps going, and the walls to either side of him turn and turn again and the lane follows, and walking along it is almost like a game of hopscotch, or finding his way blindfolded through a maze, and then it all stops. The walls fall back away from him and he is standing in the open again. There is room to stand, to stretch his arms out and breathe deeply, and there is light, there is sunlight trickling down from up above.

The lane has come to an end and here is a courtyard, and here is Luca standing where the lane ends, just before it empties itself out into this open space. There is a door on the far side of it, across from where Luca is standing—it is almost as if the jumble of all the buildings he has been walking through has drawn back from this space, to stay a respectful distance from this door and the light hanging above it. There is a tree growing here, in the middle of the courtyard; it is a spindly thing and stretched far too thin, it has too few leaves and its branches can only almost reach the light coming down from the small square of sky above it, but it really is a tree. Luca comes closer to it and he sees there is someone else here, sitting under the tree and looking up at it. He is young, like Luca, they might be the same age and he might be taller or perhaps he is shorter, Luca cannot tell because he is sitting and because of how he is sitting with his legs crossed beneath him. He sits and he looks up at the tree and then down to his lap, where he has balanced a sketchbook on his legs. There are pages torn out of it on the ground near him; some he has drawn on and others he has not and he is drawing the tree, how its trunk and its branches reach up and up and he does not stop drawing where the tree stops, he stretches the branches out into lines that run into the sky and he would keep going if he had actually reached up into the sky but he has not, he has come to the edge of the page and he stops. It seems to have stumped him. He looks up at the tree and he looks down at his sketchbook, he chews on the end of his pencil and he frowns.

When Luca comes out of the lane the other boy does not stop chewing on the end of his pencil but he is not thinking so much about drawing anymore. He is watching Luca with his head tilted a little to one side, Luca sees him and he wonders if he should say hello, and whether he was going to or not does not matter, before Luca decides what to do the boy looks back down to his drawing—he tries to draw another branch budding from a branch he has already drawn but it does not look quite right either, though he could not say why. He stops and he looks up again and he says, I'm trying to draw what the tree will be. His name is Sasha, though he does not tell Luca this, he will tell him later but not now, not yet. He has freckles across the bridge of his nose and he is wearing an old shirt that is only haphazardly buttoned, and because it is summer he is not wearing much else besides that. He asks Luca if he is looking for the college and Luca says yes, he is. Sasha smiles and points with his pencil to the door on the far side of the courtyard. It is an old door set deep into the wall, there are steps made of stone leading up to it and the light above it is set inside an elaborate curlicue of a fixture jutting out from the wall. Luca looks up at the door and then looks back at Sasha, he wants to say thank you, or something like it, but Sasha has already gone back to drawing and so he does not. He goes across the courtyard and up the steps leading to the door, there are five of them and then here is the door, and because it is an old door it is a heavy door, it sits solidly shut and Luca has to lean his weight into it to get it to open, and when it has opened enough for him to slip through he slips through and with that he is here. He has arrived at the Benjamenta College of Art.

Part One

*I*nside the college Luca has a room, and inside the room is a bed with a metal frame and a thin mattress on it; when he arrived there were sheets and a blanket and a pillow for it already here and waiting for him, folded neatly and placed on the bed, and across from the bed is a desk, the kind of desk that would be in a classroom except that it is here and not in a classroom, and at the foot of the bed is a chest of drawers and beside the chest of drawers is the door. It is a flimsy door that does not close properly and opens too easily, and when it opens there are stairs on the other side of it—to one side the stairs go up and to the other they go down, and they twist around themselves as they go up and down and all along them are other doors that lead into other rooms like this one. They all have a bed and a desk inside them, and a chest of drawers or shelves, and every once in a while, almost as if by accident, there is an actual closet. They are heaped together, these rooms, they are heaped one on top of another on top of the college and when the college is in session this is where the students live, this is where they go at the end of the day, after classes have ended and they have eaten their suppers, this is where they go when it is time to sleep.

Sometimes Luca hears the other students who live in the other rooms. He has not seen them, not yet, but he hears them when they are in their rooms, and in the morning when they go down the stairs and then in the evening when they come back up again, and at night, before he falls asleep, when it is dark and he is lying in the bed with his legs curled up under the blanket, he wonders who they are and what they are like, which of them are asleep and who stays up late, if there is anyone else lying in bed and waiting and waiting for sleep to come. There is a window over the bed that looks out onto a street, and the windows in some of the other rooms also look out onto this street and the rest of them either look out onto the roof of the college or they look out onto the roof of a building next to the college. In Luca's room there is only one curtain over the window; it covers half of the window and there should be another to cover the other half but there is not, so in the day the room fills with light and at night, when he is trying to fall asleep, the street lights shine up onto the ceiling. He lies in his bed and he watches how the light changes when a car drives by, and then in the morning, when he wakes up, the room is already full of light.

While he slept he slipped out from under the blanket, because it is still much too warm at night to be sleeping under a blanket; he likes to fall asleep curled up under it, because it feels so much better to fall asleep curled up under a blanket, and then by the morning he is sprawled out on top of it with his legs stretched across the bed and one foot hanging over the edge of it. When he is about to wake up that foot twitches, his legs stir and then he lifts his head, he looks up toward the window and the sun coming in through it and he lies like that, with his head on the pillow and looking up into the light, and he is awake but he is not entirely awake, he still has to gather up the pieces of himself from where sleeping has tossed them. His hair is tangled and messy in ways it only ever is after he has slept on it, and the window is open, the curtain sways back and forth in the breeze coming into the room and beyond it the street is already awake and moving. The cafés are open and the smell of freshly brewed coffee wafts out from their doors, a truck trundles slowly along with deliveries in the back, it stops here and there to unload a crate or two into a waiting shop and then it carries on, and up in his room Luca has sat up in the bed. He runs his fingers through his hair to work some of the tangles out, not all of them but maybe enough for it to lie flat, and then he tries to sweep all of it to one side and it will not stay like that for long, it will be back to looking like a shaggy mess soon enough but it will do for now. He swings his legs out of the bed and stands up, though not all of the way up, there is still too much sleep in him to stand all the way up; he stands up some of the way and he teeters as he works out how to stand up the rest of the way, he straightens his legs and stretches his arms out to let the sleep drain from him, and now his eyes are properly open, he is standing and awake and now to get dressed. His clothes are mostly in the chest of drawers at the foot of the bed, they should all be in the chest of drawers but some of them have found their way to the floor—a few t-shirts and some stray socks, a pair of underwear that wound up kicked under the bed and a pair of jeans near the foot of it—more will find their way there soon, soon the floor will be littered with clothes but not yet, he has not been here long enough for that. He opens a drawer and rummages through it, and while he rummages some socks fall out and onto the floor and he does not seem to notice; he closes the drawer and he opens another, he searches inside this drawer and this time he finds something. It is a t-shirt that is worn thin and ragged at the edges, he takes it out of the drawer and he holds it up for a moment to look at it and no, not this one, he stuffs it back into the drawer and he takes out another and this one he pulls over his head and down over his body and then he bends down to pick up the pair of jeans from the floor. He sits on the edge of the bed and he pulls them over one foot and then the other, he stands up to pull them the rest of the way up and his sneakers are over here by the door. He steps into them, one foot and then the other, and he opens the door, he goes out and he closes it behind him and on the other side of it is the day, waiting for him.

Everything that happens in a day happens and, when the last of it is done and over with and he has had his supper, he makes his way back up the stairs and here is his door again, he opens it and he comes through and it is dark now, or at least it almost is, the light from the street below comes up through the window and plays across the ceiling and it makes the room only almost dark, or just dark enough that Luca cannot quite see what is here. He reaches out with a hand and fumbles for the light switch, he knows it is here on the wall, to the left of the door, it is just that he is not yet sure exactly where; he feels for it and does not find it, he reaches a little higher and here it is, and over his head a light bulb dangling from a cord stutters and flickers, as if it were startled, and then a light takes hold inside it and spills out into the room and it is not so dark anymore. He takes off one of his shoes and then the other and he leaves them here, by the door, where they were in the morning and where they will be when he wakes up again, he unbuttons his jeans and he sits down on the bed to pull them most of the way off, so that they are bunched around his ankles, then he wriggles one foot free and then the other, and when his jeans are off and lying rumpled on the floor he straightens his legs out and he stands up. His legs are bare and his knees are knobbly and the t-shirt he is still wearing he has had forever, it is why it is so ragged, it is why almost all of his clothes are so ragged. It is too small for him now, there was a time when it was not and now it is too short and stretched too tight over his shoulders, now that they are wider, but no matter. He will wear it until it falls apart completely and he absolutely cannot wear it anymore and then he will figure out something else.

He is standing beside the bed and here is the desk facing him, and on the desk is a lamp with a lampshade sitting crookedly on it and beside it is a jar with pencils and pens and some brushes propped up in it, and beside the jar is a haphazard pile of books from the college library, most of them he had to borrow for his classes and then there are some that he liked the look of and so he took those too, and somewhere in among them is a sketchbook. If he were not here he would not have left it out on the desk, it would have been in a drawer or under the desk or even under the mattress of the bed but it is different here, he is not afraid of who might find it or what they might think, here there is not anything he would have to try to explain and not quite be able to, because this is what is done here, there is nothing unusual about it and so there is no more need to hide anything away for fear of what someone might think. He picks up the sketchbook from where it is on the desk and a pencil from the jar and the lead in the pencil is broken, he puts it back and he takes another and he props himself up on his elbows in the bed with his sketchbook open in front of him.

His head is bent close to it and the page stretches wide open before him and he draws, and anything could happen here on the page, or at least as much as anything he draws could be said to happen; if he keeps his eyes close to the page, if he throws himself into what he is drawing then it is happening in some way or another, and so far in his life that is as close to something happening as he has ever come. He lies in his bed and he draws, and what he draws is what he wishes would happen, like he has always done; before he came here he wished for something more than that, for something that really mattered to happen, and that is why he came here, because things are supposed to be different here, and yet here he is and he is still waiting to be swept up in something, something more, and he knows he is being impatient, he knows he has not been here long and there is still so much time for everything to happen but he cannot help himself, he does not want to wait. He wants whatever is going to happen to happen now, even if it is only in the pages of his sketchbook, so he lies in his bed and he draws like he always has, and it is dark outside and he is tired, his eyes are drooping, it is getting harder to keep them open and he is going to fall asleep with the light still on and he should not fall asleep with the light still on. He pushes himself up, so he is sitting, he slips one leg out of the bed and then the other, he finds the floor with his feet and he stands, he crosses the room and here is the light switch and now it is dark, except for the light that is not quite enough coming in through the window and playing across the ceiling. He stumbles back to the bed and the bed is against the wall, there is not enough room for it to be anywhere else, and on the other side of the wall Luca hears someone else who is still awake, still moving around. He touches the wall gently, with only the tips of his fingers, and he whispers good night to whoever it might be, he pulls the blanket over his body and he draws his legs up close, he closes his eyes and his mouth almost opens, his breath comes slower, and slower, his toes reach out to touch the foot of the bed as he sinks into sleep and then it is the morning again. He lifts his head from the pillow, he untangles his legs from the blanket and he sits up in the bed, he stretches his arms up over his head and he yawns and it is supposed to make him feel more awake when he does this but it is still much too early to be anything at all like awake, the breeze drifting in the window has too much of a chill left in it from the night before and he swings his legs out of the bed anyway, he drags himself up out of the bed and he stands. His skin prickles in the too-sharp morning air and he is already wearing a t-shirt because he fell asleep wearing it, it twisted around his body while he slept and he fidgets inside to straighten it, and all he needs to do is to find his jeans and maybe a sweater and then he will be dressed.

He scratches his head and he looks around and his jeans should be here, somewhere, but he does not see them, he pokes at the piles of clothes on the floor with his toes and they are not here, he kneels to look under the bed and there they are, half under it. He fishes them out, puts them on, and because he slept lying on his side some of the hair on that side of his head is sticking up and other parts are matted down and there is nothing he can do about that, he does not have the time; he has slept in and he has to leave right away, he has to slip on his shoes and open the door and here are the stairs, he closes his door behind him and he goes down and around and around and the steps are old, they creak painfully under him, and when they were not old they were haphazardly made so there is not much else they have ever done but creak. The rooms up here above the college are rickety things, they groan and they shift and at the top of the stairs is a window, light trickles in through it and dribbles down the stairs and it is not ever cleaned, or if it is cleaned it has been a long time since the last time and the light coming through it is dirty, and thick with grime, and Luca goes around and around and as he goes down there is a weight that settles around him, the walls become more solid, the steps more sure; he does not feel the wind on the other side of the walls and where there was wind he can feel the college settling into place and almost at the bottom of the stairs, not all the way to the bottom but almost—the stairs go down deep into the college, to the washrooms and the cellars and where the kitchens are and he does not want to go that far down, but here, almost at the bottom of the stairs, is the door that leads into the college proper.

It is no different to look at than any of the other doors along this stairwell, or if it is different it is a bit heavier, or a bit thicker, and Luca pushes on it and it opens and he goes through it and here is the college. He is in the middle of one of the corridors that wind through it, the walls here are painted a flat white and the floor is scuffed and he could go to the left or the right and he goes to the left, and here are other corridors crossing paths with this one on their way to other parts of the college, he does not know where, exactly, there are a great many places here he has not been and he does not think that he will go to all of them, or even very many of them, in the time he is here. He is not even all that sure where the corridor he is walking down now will go but he walks anyway, and there are more doors along the walls, and through them are other corridors, or rooms, there is no end to the rooms here, or of ways to find them, the college is an endless puzzle box of one kind of a room opening onto another with yet another just beyond it. It was not a building built to be a college, once it was something else, once its rooms were parlours with curtains and studies lined with books and other treasures and now they are not, some are classrooms and others are not but mostly they are one kind of classroom or another, even if they do not quite seem like it. They have been what they are now for years but still there are traces of what they were before, sometimes there is wooden trim around the doors and the windows, it was once stained and polished to a shine, or sometimes a room is wallpapered with leaves and flowers that are fading and peeling away—a kind of loving disrepair has settled over this place, something like the tenderness a grandmother might show to the children always tangled up in her skirts.

The corridor Luca is following goes this way and that through the spaces between and behind these rooms, it is how the servants would get from one room to another, back when there were servants to do what it was that the servants did; it winds past room after room and here it forks, and he turns and turns again and he is nearly where he is supposed to be. There is supposed to be a door here, and a stairwell beyond it, and there is a door here and so far so good, but instead of the stairs he was expecting to find here is the library on the other side of it. There are shelves of all different heights, some are wood and others are metal and some are a mix of both, and they are arranged in mismatched rows stretching away from the door and all of them are heavy with books, there are so many books that even the air here is weighed down by them. The librarian is somewhere inside, walking slowly among the shelves, pushing a cart of books ahead of her and every now and then she will place a volume in its proper place. Near the door that Luca has come in is a clearing with desks set out in it; they are desks like the desk in Luca's room, they are here so students have a place to sit when they are studying and around them the books gather in sombre stillness, as if any sound that might be made would be soaked up by all these pages and lost in them, and there is someone here, someone sitting with all these books sitting watchfully around her. Her head is bowed over a book, and her hair is thick and dark, it curls all on its own into ringlets and if she were standing it would tumble over her shoulders and all the way down her back but because she is sitting at a desk and bending over a book it does not. She has swung it all to one side instead, so that it falls over one shoulder and it almost but does not quite reach her lap—it is long but not that long—and the door opens, and here is Luca standing in the doorway, and the girl sitting at the desk looks up. She blinks her eyes, like someone who did not expect to be woken up but has been anyway, and they see one another, and her mouth almost moves, like it would almost move if she were talking in her sleep; she almost says hello, and she very nearly says that Luca looks lost, and does he need help but she does not say anything. Neither of them says anything, this is a library, after all, it would not be proper to be speaking in anything but a whisper and they are too far from one another for that to work. Instead Luca smiles sheepishly and he shrugs in a way that means he is sorry for making a bother of himself, it is just that he is a little bit lost, and a half smile had started to form in the corners of the girl's mouth but Luca has already gone. He has left and closed the door behind him and there is nothing to be said, not now, at least. That was Amalia, and later she will tell Luca that she remembers the lopsided way he smiled, and how he was careful to close the door quietly behind him; she will tell him and it will mean something then, but not yet, for now there is nothing to be said. She lowers her head and she looks for where she had been in her book before the door opened and Luca is back in the corridor that is clearly not the corridor he thought it was; he goes back the way he came and he turns where he was supposed to have turned the first time and he comes to another door, and on the other side of this door is the stairwell he is looking for. It is a narrow and rickety thing, this flight of stairs; it looks like a closet was taken out and stairs put in its place, and because there had not been quite enough room for the stairs Luca has to duck his head as he climbs, and at the top of the stairs is a ladder that goes up through the ceiling and at the top of the ladder is a trap door, he pokes his head up through it and here is the sky.

He has found his way up onto the roof of the college.

Once the college was not a college, it was a grand old house sitting in the middle of a quiet estate on the outskirts of the city, and it lived the life of a grand old house with picnics and tea and long evenings in front of the fire with novels that went on forever, not ending but blending imperceptibly into a gentle nodding off in a comfortable armchair, and this was life until the city grew and swallowed it up. The house vanished inside a city block, and once it had vanished it was no longer a grand old house, it was no longer a house of any kind at all. Whoever had lived there had moved away, or died, or moved away and then died, and there was nobody to think of anything else to do with it. It sat and it mouldered forgotten while around it the city carried on as if the house had never been there at all. Shops moved into the rooms that faced the street—there were streets built round it where once there had only been hedges and the occasional manicured tree—and in the back there was still the lane that led to it but the gate was locked, the key was lost and for years that was that. And now it is a college of art. Someone had found the deed to the house; it had been in an attic in a box in among any number of once important and since forgotten documents, or locked away in a safety deposit box in the vaults of some venerable old bank, unreachable because the key to it had gone missing under mysterious circumstances no one could quite remember, or perhaps it had been tucked carefully away in the top drawer of a desk but had been lost anyway in the tumult following an untimely death. But it was found, that was what mattered, and shortly after an heir as well. The house had been her grandfather's house, and she may once have visited it as a child, for a holiday or a family reunion or some other occasion she no longer remembered and somehow, for some bizarrely convoluted reason no one seemed to entirely understand, the house was hers now. The deed arrived by courier and she did not have the key to the gate but there was no need for it, the deed was enough. The gate was forced, and has not shut properly since, she went up the lane to the house with long sure strides and her skirts billowing around her, and she had no need of a grand old house, she had already had her fill of grand old houses and all of the trappings that came with them. If it had been her brother who inherited the house he likely would have made it into something like a school for servants but for her all of that was nonsense, she wanted nothing more to do with it or anything like it. She wanted something else and so she had it made into a college of art, and she became the principal.

From the streets around it there is no sign of the college but from up here, where Luca is perched on top of it, with its gabled roofs stretching out in every direction around him and chimneys poking up from wherever there was need for one, and windows looking out from attics and rooms that had been attics but have been put to other, better uses, from up here it is hard to believe that such a grand and massive thing could be so entirely hidden away. There are places where changes had to be made for the college to become a college; there are windows that had to be larger and ceilings that had to be raised, and rooms like the room Luca sleeps in that had to be built somewhere and so here they are stacked up on top of the roof—from here they look almost like the shoots of young trees pushing their way clumsily up from the ground—and in the distance, where it looks like all the gabled peaks gather and meet, Luca can see what almost looks like a glass palace. It is the glass of the skylight that looks down into the great hall in the very middle of the college, where all the college's winding corridors and hallways lead eventually, and Luca will find his way there soon but not now, not yet. For now, Luca comes out from the trap door that leads up to the roof and he comes out onto the roof, and the shingles under his feet are not solid, he has to step carefully to keep from slipping. He has his sketchbook with him, and because it is still early the sun is still drowsy and the light playing over the roof is not yet sure of itself, it floats tentatively and there are pockets of shadows here and there, left untouched, and Luca finds a place to sit, he opens his sketchbook and starts to draw. It is an assignment all new students do, they come up here, they perch somewhere in among all the peaks of the roof and they draw what they see. It is to practice drawing landscapes.

Luca thought he would be drawing rolling hills and trees against the blue of the sky but of course not, that is not what the landscape is here. What he draws is the lines of the roof stretching away from him, and the neat rows of shingles, and beyond them the city, and how the city runs up against the college and how there is no sense to how it does, or at least no sense that he can see. No two buildings look like they should have been built next to one another and yet somehow they were, and everything crowds up against everything else; the buildings do not mean to, it is just that there is not enough room to do anything else and so that is what they do. From the street it is just too bewildering for Luca to make any sense of it, it is too unlike anywhere he has ever been before but from up here it is different. He thinks he can see how it happens, how everything does what it does and how it somehow ends up fitting together, and he tries to draw that but it does not quite work out. If he looks closely enough to make sense of this part of it here, where the stairs down to the subway come up through the sidewalk and people come up and go down, then another bit of it slips away from him over there and then everything falls apart again, so instead of trying to draw everything he draws the point where two wings of the grand old house come together, where the peaks of the two roofs meet. It is where his room is, or at least it is where there is a teetering stack of rooms like the one where his room is, and where it sprouts from the roof the shingles had to part and give way and he draws how that happened, how the tiles bunch up awkwardly against it and then gradually settle back into being neatly arranged like they should be. Beyond that—it is not clear in his drawing, it is very faint, like a haze resting on a distant horizon even though it is not that far away—he has left a space for the restless jumble of the rest of the city. He draws just enough of it to hint that it is there, the peaks of roofs here and there, the spaces between them where there are streets, and perhaps that is the best that could be done, and no matter if it is or not, it does not make a difference, he has run out of time. He looks at what he has done and he thinks he is pleased, and he stands up, and because it is awkward and not at all comfortable to be drawing while perched on the top of a roof there are kinks that have worked themselves into his back and his legs and as he stands he stretches to work them out. He raises his arms up over his head and his spine gradually unclenches itself and he takes a last look at the sky and the city spread out around him, except that it is not quite around him. He is still in the middle of it, of course, but distantly, there is space and nothing but space around him and it has been so long since he has been out in the open like this. It reminds him of where he came from and for a moment, just for a moment, he misses it—he misses how wide open the sky is and how peaceful it is, having what feels like the whole world spread out before him; he breathes in just a little more of this wide open feeling and then he bends to open the trap door he came up through. He lifts it up and he holds it up with one hand while he reaches with one foot for the top rung of the ladder, he puts his weight onto it and he twists around to put his other leg through, he lowers himself down and he climbs down the ladder and he is at the top of the stairs again, and as he goes back down and into the college the sprawling mess of it settles comfortably back into place around him.

It is the evening or it is almost the evening, because it is hard to say exactly when a day ends and an evening begins, Luca has spent the whole of the day drawing up on the roof and now he is hungry, and somewhere in the college supper is waiting for him. Here is the corridor that goes back the way he came in the morning; it goes to the stairs that go to his room and he does not go that way, he almost does but he remembers in time and he turns and goes down into another part of the college instead. He goes down a different flight of stairs and at the bottom of these stairs he comes out into another corridor going off to wherever it is that it goes, Luca is never quite sure where any of the corridors go and somehow he does not get lost, or at least he does not get lost that often, and when he does he is almost always pleasantly surprised to have somehow arrived wherever he was supposed to arrive anyway. He follows this corridor along and the floor creaks under him, and he wonders if it is because of him but he need not worry, the college's aches and pains are its own and its own alone and they will carry on acting up with or without him. He winds through the college, he goes one way and then another through one kind of corridor and then another; he goes up one flight of stairs and then down another and sometimes he doubles back on himself but it cannot be helped, he does not know a better way to get to where he is going.

Sometimes he walks past another student, or another student will walk past him on their way to wherever it is they are going, and all that happens is a jostling of elbows and Luca would like there to be more than that but he does not know anyone here, none of these faces are familiar and then one of them is. He passes someone and he thinks that he remembers him, that he saw him outside the day he arrived and he says, hello, and he asks this other boy if he is who he thinks he is and the other boy tilts his head and he looks at Luca closely and he says yes, he remembers him. He says hello, he says that his name is Sasha and he is on his way down to the kitchens, for supper, and so is Luca, and since they are both on their way to the same place why don't they walk together. Luca is not entirely sure how to get there so it is Sasha who leads them, they walk down a corridor that Luca does not think he has gone down before, he is about to say something but Sasha says to trust him and they stop in front of a particular door that does not seem to be any different than any of the other doors along this corridor—some of them open onto rooms that are being used as classrooms but most of them are not, the rooms behind them are not being used for anything, they still are what they were before except for the time that passed by without them being used. The door Sasha opens is one of those doors, it leads to a room that was once a sitting room, or something like a sitting room; Luca does not know what it would have been called but whatever it was, it was what he would imagine a sitting room to be. Here is a sofa, with armchairs to either side of it and a low table in front of them and another table, a smaller table, with two chairs tucked under it by the window and none of them have been sat in for ages. There are cloths draped over them and dust lying thick over the room and in the dust is a path going from one side of the room to the other. Sasha opens the door and they are on one side of the room and there is a door on the other side and Sasha says, it's a shortcut, this place is full of them, and he leads Luca through the door and along the path through the dust and they come out on the other side and they are that much closer to the great hall, much closer than Luca thought they possibly could be; they go a little bit further and turn to their left, they go through a door and then there they are.

The great hall would be a magnificently grand room if there was not too much of it to feel like a room, so instead of being a room it is a great open space in the middle of the college, it is its heart and all the rest of it radiates out from this place. There is a staircase at one end sweeping up toward a pair of ornate double doors, and a balcony circling entirely around it and up overhead the ceiling is a skylight, and during the day the hall is flush with light and now that it is the evening—or it is almost the evening or not quite the evening, it is still hard to say—the light feels thicker, and heavier, like it too is tired after a long day and settling sleepily into the corners for the night. Luca and Sasha come into the hall and all the other students are coming from all over the college, they come one after another and sometimes two or three will arrive together, they may have had a class together, or they may have met on their way here, and they all come into the great hall and they all come to this one particular door on the other side of the hall. It is nearly hidden away in a far corner and they go through it one after another and then they are where the servants' quarters were, which is why the door was tucked out of the way, and a little further on is the door that leads out to the lane behind the college and below them are the kitchens. Luca and Sasha are walking behind a girl with raggedy hair that is only almost pinned up, most of it is but there are bits sticking out around her ears and trailing down her neck and there are other people in front of them and even more behind them and they all go down a flight of bare wooden steps together and here are the kitchens. They are like they always were—people still eat, that will never change, and so the kitchens have not changed either, there are stovetops and giant pots simmering and cooks bustling about, and the cooks are all at the far end of the kitchens, where the cooking is done, and at the bottom of the stairs there are three long tables set out, one in the middle of the room and the others beside it, and benches alongside them and this is where the students come, this is where they eat. They come down the stairs and they come into the kitchens and on the other side of the tables, in between them and where all the cooks are bustling about, there is a counter where there are trays and plates and bowls and a vast assortment of mismatched cutlery waiting, and another counter with a pot of stew and thick slices of bread and butter and cooks waiting behind the pots with ladles in hand. Luca takes a tray and a bowl and a plate and he puts two slices of bread on his plate, he holds out his bowl for a cook to ladle stew into it and with all this balanced on his tray he goes looking for a place to sit.

Sasha has already vanished into the crowd and all the tables are filling up with students and their bowls of stew, there are more students coming down the stairs and those already here are looking for places to sit and soon all the places to sit will be taken. Luca walks with his tray held high, so that no one accidentally bumps it, and he sees a girl with curly red hair streaming from her head and next to her a boy with large hands and a spoon that seems far too small nestled in one of them, he holds it carefully between two fingers and he bends his head down close to his bowl, to keep from spilling, and there is just enough room left for Luca between them. He puts his tray on the table and he sits on the bench and all around him everyone is talking, and the ruckus of it rises up over the sounds of dishes clattering and the cooks bustling about and he catches little bits of what is being said—there are people talking about assignments from classes he has not even heard of yet, they are talking about paint like it is light falling through coloured glass, or paint with bits of glass mixed into it and light falling through that, he cannot quite tell and he tries to listen in, no matter that it is not the best of manners but he cannot help himself, he wants to know what he might end up doing. The girl who is sitting beside him, the one with red hair, is talking about a meeting she just came from, with one of the tutors, and how they are trying to figure out how to make a painting feel like it smells like something, what it would have to look like to feel like it smells like something, or maybe even how to make it actually smell like something, what kind of paint would she have to make, and Luca cannot help but also wonder while he sits quietly and eats his stew. He eats spoonful after spoonful without saying a word and he listens, he listens to everything he can and when he is stuffed full of it he mops up the last bits of his stew with his last bit of bread and when it is gone he takes his tray and his bowl to where he is supposed to take them, he puts them on a counter, and one of the cooks whisks them away to be washed and put away, and he makes his way out of the kitchens and back up into the college above. It is dark now, and it is definitely the evening if it is not already night and Luca is in the great hall again. There are lights here now, or there always were but now they are lit, and Luca can see them; they are held in elaborately filigreed fixtures that reach out from the walls like cupped hands, there is no need of them in the day when the sun is pouring in but now there is, and so there are little islands of light floating in the dark around them. Luca steps from the dim of the corridor into a half-light and then back into the dark; he picks his way carefully through the middle of the hall and out the far side of it and here is a corridor plunging back into the college, it takes him to another corridor and he turns without first thinking whether he should or not—he is coming close to being able to do this easily, at last he is starting to figure out how this place works. He still does not entirely know where he is going but he wanders along and a couple of twists and turns later, with only a very little doubling back, and here he is at the foot of the stairs going up to his room. He grabs hold of the banister and he goes up one step and then another and somewhere up above him is the sound of what might be someone else going up the stairs. He goes past one door and then another and every one is different, they are all different sizes and made from all different kinds of wood, when they are made of wood, and not even the door handles are ever the same, and even though he hurries Luca does not see who was ahead of him. There may not even have been someone there, it might have been nothing, a sound the stairs make all on their own no matter how badly someone might wish otherwise. There is light bleeding out from under some of the doors and sometimes he can hear people on the other sides of them but all he can see as he goes up and around are doors and the stairs going up and around the emptiness of the stairwell. If he looked over the banister he would see all the way down to the cellars but he does not, he goes up and around some more until at last he comes to the door to his room.

Inside it is dark, and in the dark he reaches for the switch on the wall to turn on the light, it is getting easier for him to find it in the dark, and he switches it on and the bulb over his head flickers and then it is light in the room. He unbuttons his shirt, he is wearing a shirt that buttons up today, and he had buttoned it all the way up because he thought it would look smart but he did not like how it pressed on his throat so he unbuttoned some of the buttons and now he unbuttons the rest and he lets it drop to the floor, he unbuttons his jeans and he sits on the bed to take them off and his hair is sticking up in ways he wishes it did not. His sketchbook is on top of the chest of drawers at the foot of the bed—he remembered to put it somewhere last night, before he fell asleep, and he turns and he reaches for it and he lies down with it and here is a blank page before him and he draws, and it makes him less lonely or it makes his loneliness matter less, because he is lonely, even with everything happening around him and how exciting it all is, and it almost makes him want to cry but he does not, because what if he just needs to wait a little more, what if he is just tired, what if he only needs to sleep. His eyes droop and his hand slows and as he falls asleep he rolls over, so he is lying on his back; his chest rises and falls and he is asleep with his sketchbook still lying open beside him, and this is what life is now. It is not what it was—he did not stretch out into sleep before he came here, he curled himself around it, like he had to keep it safe, and what he dreamt he kept hidden away and here the street beneath his window moves but it moves softly, quietly, so as not to disturb anyone sleeping above it. The light that comes in through the window touches the ceiling gently, and as he sleeps his legs slowly stretch out, his toes touch the foot of the bed and this is what it is like here, this is what it is like to be here.

—

In the morning the sun comes up and Luca is still asleep, because it is far too early to be awake when the sun first comes up; his pillow is somewhere other than under his head and he is lying on his stomach and one of his legs stretches out one way and the other is tangled in his blankets, and they are both not quite but almost moving, as if there is something happening inside his sleep. Later, when he does wake up, he raises his head and he feels for his pillow and it is not there—it rarely is, but he always feels for it, and his eyes are not quite open yet so he searches the bed with his hands and he finds it under one of his legs, and he would like to curl around it and fall back asleep but he puts it back where it should be at the head of the bed, he untangles himself from the blankets and he sits up. His hair is a knotted mess and he tries to run his fingers through it but it is too tangled for that to do much of anything, he does his best anyway and it is still a mess after but enough of it is out of his face and lying mostly flat that he can stop thinking about it and that is enough for now. He swings his legs out from the bed and he stands up, and then wobbles from having stood up too quickly and too soon after waking up. He steadies himself and then he reaches down to pick up his jeans from the floor by the foot of the bed, and here is a t-shirt he tossed over the back of the chair at his desk a couple of days ago, and here are a mismatched pair of socks he hopes are not too dirty to wear again; he puts all of them on, one after another, and then his sneakers and once he has his sneakers on he is out the door and going down the stairs, and here is the door almost at the bottom of them. He goes through it and then another, and any number of corridors between the two and here he is in the great hall, and overhead up above the skylight there are wisps of cloud skittering across the blue of the sky, and light, there is so much light pouring down. Only a trickle comes in through the window in his room and this is so much he wants to close his eyes, he wants to turn his face up and soak himself in it, and he almost stops and he almost does but then he is across the hall and going down the stairs to the kitchens. It is not as busy now as it sometimes is, it is much too early for that and there are only a few students standing in line and waiting for their turn to get breakfast, and at the head of the line are the cooks serving sausages and eggs, or oatmeal, or cut fruits arranged in a bowl, or toast with jam spread on it and thick slices of cheese, and beyond them other cooks are bustling about over the stoves. Some come carrying bowls or pots or steaming platters and others come to take them away when they are empty, and the students arrive at the head of the line with their plates at the ready and they come away with them piled high. When Luca's turn comes one cook asks him if he would like hard-boiled eggs or soft, and he says soft, please, and here are two of them, still in their shells; another cook puts two slices of toast on his plate and he pours himself a cup of tea and with his breakfast in hand he turns to look for a place to sit.

Sasha is here, he is sitting near to the end of one of the tables, and now that they have met properly and introduced themselves to one another they are something like friends; they say hello when they see one another and they will sit together in the kitchens, sometimes, if there is room, and there is room so Luca sits beside him. Sasha looks up to say hello and then he goes back to peeling the shells from his eggs, he has been here longer than Luca, he is in his last year and sometimes when they sit together Luca does not want to say or do anything, he just wants to watch what Sasha does and how he talks and learn what he should do. He is sitting next to Sasha and sitting across from them but not quite across from them, across and a little to the left is a girl with a single egg and a slice of bread on the plate in front of her and behind that girl are two people sitting closer together than anyone else is sitting. One has her arm around the other's hips and they are whispering to one another and only to one another, and it is like everyone else is small or far away, or like they have slipped away into one another, to where no one else can see them even though everyone can, and seeing them together and how easily they sit together makes Luca's heart twinge. He looks away and he breaks the shell of one of his eggs against his plate and peels it away with his fingers, if there was a salt shaker on the table he would sprinkle a bit of salt on it but there is not so he takes a bite of it and yolk comes slopping out, he catches it with his tongue and he licks it up, and then he takes another bite and that is nearly all of it gone. He puts down the little that is left, he licks a bit of yolk off his fingers and he picks up a slice of toast and the girl who was sitting across from him has gone and Amalia is sitting where the girl had been. She is not leaning over a book this time, she is sitting up straight and she has her breakfast on a tray in front of her and a smile almost playing in the corners of her mouth—it is nearly always there, that smile, it is the shape her mouth makes and it makes it hard to tell when she is actually smiling and when she is not. Luca takes a bite from his slice of toast and it leaves behind a bit of butter on his cheek, he wipes it away and he looks up and he recognizes Amalia, he is not sure from where but he does, and she almost smiles, in the way that she does, and he is not sure if it really is a smile or if it is not and he is not entirely sure he recognizes her. It may only be that he wishes he does and he does not know if he should smile, or say anything, or not.

They sit across from one another and they eat and sometimes Luca looks up at Amalia and sometimes Amalia looks across the table at Luca and once their eyes meet, and it is an accident, they both look at the same time and their eyes meet and neither of them says a thing, because what could they say, they do not know one another yet. Luca looks away and he puts the last of his toast in his mouth and Amalia has a bowl of cereal with berries on top and Luca wishes for something to say—he has finally remembered where he saw Amalia before, and he wonders what she might have been reading and if he can ask her and he does not, he does not quite have the courage to; he finishes his breakfast and he takes his tray and he stands up, he leaves his tray where he is supposed to leave it and he leaves, and as he leaves he steals a last glance at Amalia. She sits with her bowl of cereal in front of her and Luca does not see it but from the corner of her eye Amalia watches as he walks from one end of the kitchen to the other and then up the stairs, and then he has come up from the kitchens and here is the great hall, here is the staircase in the middle of it, leading up to the balcony overhead, and here at the top of the staircase are the double doors that open onto what might have been a dining room but now it is the college gallery. When the students' work is done it is brought here, and when there is enough of it there is a show, and after the show that is it, the year is over, the college closes for the summer and everything is taken down to make room for the next year's work. All of that is still a while away, for now, the gallery is mostly empty—there is a picture up on the wall here and there, and a sculpture off in one corner, and a cart with things on it that have just arrived and are waiting to be put where things are put when they arrive, before they go up on the walls.

Luca comes to the top of the stairs and he goes past the gallery, he goes around the balcony circling above the great hall and past the doors leading off from it. They are not like the plain and flimsy doors in the corridors he usually walks along, they are more solid, and more ornate, more befitting the kind of place that the school was, and Luca goes from one of these doors to the next until he comes to this one and he stops, he turns the handle and he opens it, slowly, and not all the way, only enough to slip through and he is in a classroom, or rather he is in a room that was once something other than a classroom and now it is a classroom. Here are a pair of sofas and a handful of armchairs that would be better suited to tea and an idle conversation unfolding over a slow afternoon, they have been rearranged so they are all in rows facing the same way and behind them is a window that looks out over a courtyard, or maybe it is a garden, or it is what was once a garden and now it is an open space left untended and growing wild and here, at the front of the room, is one of the lecturers. He is standing at a lectern and all the chairs and the sofas and whatnot have been arranged so that they are facing him, and when Luca slips through the door there are other students already here, and when they came in the lecturer was already here, he was standing at the front of the room and he was waiting, and as the students came in they hushed and they sat, quietly, and now they are sitting here and there, some of them close together and others on their own and they are waiting too. There is a clock on the wall, behind the lecturer, and it is almost the hour but not quite, and so the class has not started yet; the lecturer stands at the front of the room and his eyes were once blue or green and now they are grey, and his eyelids are lined and heavy and all the rest of him is grey too. His lips are thin and his cheeks hollow and there is something distant about him, like he is looking down on the lectern from a great height that only the tips of his fingers cross when they rest, briefly, on the notes arranged on the lectern before him. Luca comes into the room and he looks for a place to sit, and he sits on one of the sofas and he has sat beside a girl wearing glasses. Behind her glasses her eyes look like they are open too wide and with her glasses they look even wider, and her glasses do not quite sit properly on her face, they are broken at the bridge of the nose and she has done her best to glue them back together, where they are broken there is a gob of glue, and now they sit slightly crookedly on her face and they are always about to fall down her nose. Luca smiles as he sits down—he does not smile all the way, that would be too much, he thinks, because when he smiles it is a great big thing sitting lopsidedly on his face and he tries to smile only some of the way even though he is not terribly good at smiling only some of the way. The girl's glasses have slipped down her nose and she turns away from Luca to push them back up to where they should be, and before she did she might have sort of smiled and she might not have, Luca could not quite tell. After the class they will have more to say but for now they sit next to one another and the professor lifts his wrist to look at his watch and it is the hour exactly. It is time for the class to start.

This class is an introduction to materials—it is his expertise, this lecturer; there are other lecturers who lecture on other topics and this lecturer, his specialty is materials. Somewhere in the college he has a workshop and there he has sheets and rolls and reams of nearly every type of paper there is to be found; some of his samples are old, some of them new, and he rests his fingers on them, to feel for what they were made from; he makes notes and his notes have gathered into books and there is a shelf of them there, against one of the walls, every one of them carefully bound. He spends his days there and when evening comes he takes his jacket from where it hangs on a hook behind the door, he closes up the workshop and he leaves the college, he goes to a small room in a small apartment nearby, and on his way he stops to eat in a small bistro between here and there. Almost every night he comes in, he waits at the door and he is seated at a table near the kitchen, it is always the same table, and he looks briefly at the menu, even though there is no need, he knows it by heart, but he does anyway and when someone comes to take his order he orders, and after he has ordered he rests his head in his hands, he kneads his eyelids with the tips of his fingers, and when his meal comes he eats, neatly and delicately, he looks as if he is meditating on every bite, and after he has eaten he turns to look into the kitchen. The chef looks up and their eyes meet—the chef wipes his hands on his apron, or he straightens his cap and the lecturer wipes the corners of his mouth with his napkin. Their eyes meet and they nod, first one, then the other, then the lecturer stands, he pays and he leaves, and when he arrives in his small room in his apartment he examines a book— he does not read it, or if he does it is only in passing, almost by accident, what he does is feel for how the paper has taken to being bound, how it has taken to ink, what kind of a book does it make for and later the door will open and the lecturer will look up. He will put whatever he had been looking at aside and will stand, it always comes as a surprise to him how quickly he stands and how pleased he still is that the door has opened. The chef from the restaurant is here, he has come home and they will sit together in the kitchen, they will have a drink or they will not, it depends on the night and the day that has passed, or the chef will have brought something home with him from the restaurant, and they will eat, or they will simply sit and talk and after, when it is later, when it is much, much later, they will go to bed curled up together.

Except that it is not the night, it is still the morning and here he is at the front of a class, and he has brought samples of different kinds of paper to speak about and he speaks about them and Luca follows along as best he can, which is not terribly well because he would rather have said hello to the girl sitting beside him. He wishes he had, and he keeps almost turning his head to see what she is doing, to see if she is listening or not, and when the class is over it is slightly after when the class was supposed to be over; the lecturer had lost track of time, and he was still speaking when he should have stopped. He lifts his wrist to look at his watch and his eyebrows rise, he lowers his hands and abruptly he stops, it catches Luca unawares, he blinks, and it takes him a moment to realize the lecture has ended, it is like he has just suddenly fallen back into himself and around him the other students stir and start to slowly stand up, and they look around the room like it is a bit of a surprise to them too. The ones who brought things like notebooks with them tuck them away into their bags and they start for the door but Luca does not, he turns to look at the girl sitting beside him and she has not stood either, they are still sitting beside one another and Luca turns to her and her glasses are sitting where they should be, she has just pushed them back into place and they will slip back down her nose soon enough but for now they are where they should be and she smiles, she has a small, shy smile, like she is not used to it, and Luca says hello, my name is Luca, and her name is Mattie and they stand up and they leave the room together. Mattie is smaller than Luca, and slighter, standing beside one another it looks like she could fit inside of him, and she is wearing a cardigan with all the buttons done up, and a shirt with a collar and all its buttons done up, and she is new here, like Luca is new here, and there is so much that neither of them is sure of. They do not know what to make of this place, no matter that they both wanted so badly to come, or how to feel about what they left behind when they came here. Mattie stops before she says this, she ducks her head and she pushes her glasses back up her nose even though they had not quite fallen, and after, when she speaks, it is quietly, like there is a lump in her throat when she talks about where she came from. She misses it. She had a life there and she was used to that life, to her room and her parents, she did not say much to them and they did not say much to her but they ate supper together nearly every night, she and her parents, and her school was nearby and between it and her house was a park and ever since she was little she would go to the park and even if she had her reasons for leaving—for her what was there had run out, there was nothing left for her but still she misses it, and yes, Luca knows that feeling. He lived in a neat little house with a yard around it and a car out front and a street that would have eventually led to something other than a house with a yard around it and a car out front, even if it never seemed to, and he could not imagine himself as the kind of person who would settle down to live in that kind of a house in that kind of a place, so he left, and even though he wanted to leave behind everything he left behind it still aches to be without it, to be alone here—because it is lonely here, no matter what else it is it is lonely too, and when Mattie's voice comes up against a lump Luca's heart jumps because he knows what that is like, he knows that feeling.

He does not know how to say it or even if he could say it, neither does Mattie, the closest she can come to saying how it feels is the lump in her throat and maybe they do not have to say it, maybe it is enough to have it between them and somehow to know it, even if it is not ever something either of them will ever say. Mattie tells Luca that the room she sleeps in is not one of the rooms built on top of the college, it is one of the attics, and it was too large to make just one room out of it so walls were built in the middle of it, to divide it; they only go almost all the way to the ceiling and on the other side of the walls there are other students in rooms like hers, and when they see one another, in the corridors or in the kitchens, they do not know what to say because they do not know one another, even though they know the sounds they all make when they get ready for bed, and what is there to say to someone you know like that, and when she says this she is also saying what she cannot say, and the lump in her throat slowly works itself out. Neither of them had heard of lingonberry jam before coming here, and here it is sometimes served with breakfast and they both quite like it, and they wonder where it comes from and here they are, on a landing in the middle of a flight of stairs. They have been wandering and talking, and so long as they were wandering without anywhere in particular to go there was time to say more but now that time has run out, Mattie has to go one way and Luca another. Mattie looks away, she pushes her glasses back up her nose and Luca almost steps closer to her, he wants to hold her—he imagines it would feel like holding a bird in his hand, he imagines how they would tremble and he wants to but he does not. Mattie has to go this way, to the workshops, there is something she wants to see, something that the lecturer mentioned in class, and she has to be there before supper and the afternoon is running out. They stand awkwardly, and Mattie starts to turn away and Luca says, see you later, and Mattie looks back with something like a smile and she says yes, okay. She goes down the stairs and Luca's heart is beating too much, he hopes it does not rise all the way to his cheeks and he stands and he watches Mattie slip down the stairs and at the bottom of them she vanishes, and when she has vanished Luca goes up the stairs, to where there is another lecture to attend, and then there is supper, and after supper it is dark outside, or if it is not entirely dark, because it is never entirely dark in a city, then it is closer to dark than it is to anything else and Luca makes his way back up to his room.

He is almost there, he is climbing the last of the stairs between him and his door, there are lights set into the walls to guide him—

they are dim, and they flicker, and they almost but not quite light the stairwell. If it was later Luca would slip in and out of the pools of light spilling from them but now it is only that the light is uneven, and sometimes it is bright and other times there are shadows taking root in the corners, and he goes up one last turn in the stairs and here is his door. He comes into his room and he flicks the switch to turn on the light and the bulb is bare and the light is too harsh, it makes the room and what is in the room look wrong or too exposed but it is what the light in here is. He unbuttons his jeans and he sits on the bed to take them off, he works his feet out of them and they drop to the floor and he is tired but he does not want to sleep, he does not want to stop, not yet. It feels like something has happened and he wants for something more to happen, he wants it to keep going and never stop, he wants to be carried away and lost inside it but it is late and the light is too much, it is too bright, it makes him feel too small or too naked, like if he were to curl up and fall asleep in it he would shrink away and disappear completely so he stands up, he crosses the room and he turns the light off and it is dark now. It is dark outside and dark here too and he makes his way through the dark—there are no end of things on the floor to catch his feet on and he has to step carefully back to the bed, and he lies in the dark and if only there were something other than this and of course there is not. He is a boy lying alone in the dark and there is the sound of the street outside, there are the street lights and the ceiling and it was supposed to be different here, and then he is asleep, and in the morning he remembers the books on his desk, the ones that came from the library that have to go back to the library today. Luca picks himself up out of the bed and it is colder than it was, it is autumn, it is getting colder at night and in the morning it is still cold and his skin prickles while he looks on the floor for something to wear. Here are his jeans and a t-shirt and he looks for a sweater to pull on over the t-shirt, or rather he pulls what is left of a sweater over his t-shirt—it is more holes than anything else, and what is left of it hangs loose from his body, he slips his feet into his sneakers and he leaves his room with his arms heavy with books and he is off in search of the library. There is the way he found when he was not looking for it and another he found when he was; he does not remember either of them especially well and he has only a little time, he has to go to the library and then to breakfast and after that he has a class and after that another, and the one way to the library goes round and round more often than it should and the way he found by accident is shorter, he thinks, and if it is then it will be quicker, or at least it will be quicker if he can find it again. He thinks he can find it, though, it is on the way to the roof and he remembers the way to the roof—he likes to go back there, sometimes, when he needs to feel the sky open above him—so to find the library all he has to do is get lost on the way to the roof again, and he almost makes it to the roof before he remembers what he is supposed to be doing; he is standing at the bottom of a ladder he cannot climb because his arms are full of books, he turns back and this time he remembers to turn where he did the time he got lost, and here is the library, here are the shelves and the books and the squeaky wheels on the cart the librarian pushes ahead of her when she is shelving books; Luca opens the door and here are the shelves and on the other side of them is the librarian's desk, where Luca has to go, and between here and there is Amalia.

Luca is holding his books against his chest and he comes into the library too quietly and too carefully, like he is afraid to make a sound, and Amalia is sitting at a desk with a book open in front of her. She watches as Luca opens the door and closes it behind him, it is tricky because of how many books he is carrying but he manages, and when the door is closed and Luca is sure the door is closed he turns and he sees Amalia. Amalia had looked up when the door opened, to see who had opened it, and she saw Luca and she is still looking at him with her head tilted a little to one side, and their eyes meet again, like they did in the kitchens, and it would not mean anything if they were to look away again but this time they do not. Amalia is already almost smiling, and Luca shifts the weight of the books in his arms to keep from dropping them and he smiles too, a big and lopsided grin. He has to go past Amalia to the librarian's desk to return his books, and Amalia looks back down to her book and Luca carries on to the desk, the librarian is not there and he should wait for her but he does not want to so he leaves his books where she will find them, and there is a door here that would take him on his way to breakfast and instead he goes back the way he came. Amalia is still where she was, except that she has closed the book she was reading, and when Luca comes out from the shelves Amalia turns to look at him and she smiles, there is no doubt this time, she looks at Luca and she smiles and his heart skips; one of his hands goes up to his hair, because it is probably a mess but he need not worry, somehow it is fine, and his hand drops, and Amalia says, hello. She turns in her chair toward Luca and she rests her arms on the back of it and her chin on her arms and she asks, have you had breakfast yet, and Luca says he hasn't, and because he is not sure what is happening it comes out more like a question than an answer to one and Amalia smiles further, it reaches up to her eyes and crinkles the corners of them and she asks, shall we go together.

They leave the library and they go through the college, they go through the great hall and here are the stairs going down into the kitchen but they do not go down, they go past them; Luca almost turns to go down but Amalia takes his hand and they carry on, and he is confused but he does not ask why, he is too swept up in whatever is happening to ask why. They go past the stairs and into the reception hall, there is the door they came through and another across from it that leads out of the college and between the two is the desk the secretary sits at, when he is here. There is no one here now, the secretary is likely upstairs with the records or away somewhere with the principal, or perhaps he is away somewhere without her, but no matter where he has wound up it means that there is no one to see Amalia leading Luca through the reception hall and out the other side of it. They come to the door that is the way out of the college, with a heave they push it open and they go through, one after the other, and here is the courtyard at the end of the lane, here is the sun shining down from the square of sky overhead and together they set out down the lane and into the city. The air has an autumn bite to it and it is good that Luca is wearing a sweater, and Amalia is wearing a cardigan over a dress that gathers neatly at her waist and flares out over her hips; the ends of her cardigan and her dress swing round her legs and her hair trails behind her as she walks, and they come out of the lane and into the street and Luca remembers this street, even if he cannot remember much of anything about it. This is the way he came when he first came here, he almost remembers the shops they walk past and then he does not, they have turned onto another street and this street is new to him.

There are shops along this street too but there are not only shops, there are people who live on this street, and here are the doors to their houses, overhead are the branches of trees shading the sidewalk and there are hedges between some of the doors and the street, and here are people walking along without going anywhere, as if they are out walking for the sake of being out walking, because this is where they live, and of course there are people who live here, even if Luca does not quite believe that anyone could actually live in this city—it seems like there is too much always happening for anyone to ever be able to settle into bed for a good night's sleep but here they are. They smile absently, some say good morning as they walk past, and Amalia leads Luca down this street and then another, and then on this corner is a café with tables set out on the street in front of it, and inside is someone sitting with a book and a cup of tea and nobody else. There were others who came in to get a cup of coffee before heading out into the day, and there will be others when it is time for lunch, but now there is just this one table with someone sitting at it, and the people who work here, of course. There is a cook behind the counter and a waitress, and for them this is a quiet moment to wipe down the tables and straighten the chairs before everything starts up again. Luca and Amalia come in and they sit at a table by the window, there are plants in the window, there are pots of all different sizes all along the windowsill and some have flowered but most have not, most are not even the kinds of plants that have flowers, and the waitress said hello to them as they came in and now that they are sitting she comes over with menus and Amalia will have granola with yogurt and fresh fruit on top of it please, and Luca has not ever been here before so he has to look through the menu; he looks at one page and then another and he thinks he will have waffles with whipped cream and blueberry syrup, and then he almost changes his mind but yes, he will have that after all, and the waitress nods and she writes in a small notepad, she tucks it into her apron and then she leaves Luca and Amalia sitting across from one another. For Luca it is the first time he has been out in the city—he has tried before, but every time he got no further than almost getting lost—and this is the first time he has done anything other than wander aimlessly, it is the first time he has felt like he has properly gone somewhere. He sits with his hands tucked beneath his legs and he looks out the window, he looks up and down the street, and at all the different ways there are to build a house here, and nearly everyone who walks by catches his eye and Amalia sits across from him, watching him without looking like she is watching him and smiling in the corners of her mouth. Amalia sits properly, with her shoulders straight and her elbows at her sides; she is always sure to carry herself properly and to dress properly, no matter that her dresses are always ever so slightly outlandish. If she did not have all this hair tumbling down her back there would be something too precociously ladylike to her and all this is a choice, it is a choice to be this proper, to prove she can be this proper. It is a show of strength. Her eyes sparkle now but they can be proud and hard and impossibly stubborn too, it is why her hair is as long as it is, no matter that it is a bit too much to be entirely proper and neat, and it is why she is sitting here across from Luca and his ragged sweater, with his mop of hair and a big lopsided grin lighting up his face.

Their breakfasts come and they eat, and after they eat they share a pot of tea; more people had arrived while they were eating, they have to lean closer together to hear one another over the sound of everyone else coming and going or sitting down at a table to meet a friend, they are close enough that their teacups almost touch in the middle of the table and Luca likes being this close to this girl, and Amalia is smiling too, and it is not her slight smile, she is smiling so much that she almost trips over it when she tries to speak. They drink all their pot of tea and they should leave, they both have to be back in the college and when they do eventually decide to leave it is too late, Luca has already missed a class and there is another after lunch, he should not miss that one too, so they stand and they go to the counter to pay and then they are back in the street and on their way back to the college. They walk down one street and then another, they slip through the gate and in the lane they walk closer together, and it is not only because there is not enough space to do much of anything but walk close together. The lane takes them back to the courtyard and the tree growing in it, they come back into the college and one of them is going one way and the other is not. They are still close together, and here there really is no other reason for it other than to be close enough they can feel one another as a tingling on their skin. Amalia opens her arms and Luca steps closer, he puts his arms around this girl and she is soft, she is so soft and Luca holds her too tightly or for too long and when they step away Amalia is smiling in the corners of her mouth the way that she smiles in the corners of her mouth. She says goodbye and Luca does not entirely trust himself to speak, because there are times he does not trust himself to not do what he wants to do, he grins helplessly and somehow he manages to say goodbye too.

This happens in the great hall. One of them is going to go one way and the other somewhere else and they know they are going to say goodbye but neither of them is in any rush to. When they do at last get to it, when they step too close together and hold one another too long it is in the light coming down from the skylight above; there is not any of the chill of the autumn air in it, it is warm and golden and they say goodbye, and one of them goes one way and the other somewhere else.

Part Two

*I*t is a day, it is another day and it is the middle of the day and Luca has come up to a room at the very top of the college, it was an attic once and now it is a room, a proper room, there are windows all along one of the walls and light pours in through them, it is clear and bright inside and it is a small room, even though it does not feel like a small room. The ceiling is much higher than ceilings usually are, and at the height where the ceiling should have been there is a fan instead, it hangs down into the room and it turns slowly, stirring the air and the ceiling is somewhere up above where it should have been and having all that space overhead makes the room feel more open than it actually is. Luca came up through the college and down a rickety corridor, he came in through the door and here in the room there are things piled in the corners and stacked along the walls; there does not seem to be any reason they are all here and piled together, and to look at them Luca cannot tell what any of them are, all he can make out are bits and pieces of whatever is there and all together these bits and pieces are not anything other than a heap of stuff sprawling out along all four of the walls.

Here is the door and here is the light and here are the heaps of stuff and here are two old men in the middle of the room, kneeling beside one another and muttering between themselves. They are wearing coveralls the colour of old things—they are grey or green, or almost, or they are not exactly a colour but something like grey or green, or something that was once grey or green and now they are just old and these are the caretakers. One of them has a bushy moustache and the other has whiskers, and they are kneeling in front of a table they have placed in the middle of the room and on it they are precisely arranging a vase, an alarm clock, and a jar with the parts of old watches inside. Beside them is a cart that looks as rickety and old as they do and it is weighed down with all the things they need to do what they do—there are useful things on it, like a mop and a bucket, and rags for cleaning up spills, and also a crate carefully packed with tea cups that they have gathered from all the places where tea cups are sometimes left behind. The caretakers had brought the vase that is now on the table with them, and also the alarm clock, the jar they found in a cupboard partly buried along the wall and now they are arranging all these things on the table. The alarm clock is in the middle and the vase is in front and the jar off to one side; they put it to that side then change their minds and put it on the other side instead, and then they step back from the table to look at it and mutter between themselves and they come to some kind of conclusion. They shake their heads, they go back to the table and they move the alarm clock and the jar so they are together and they put the vase off to one side, and they seem to think this is better and Luca wonders why. He has come through the door and he is standing just inside the room and he watches as they mutter between themselves and arrange and rearrange the things on the table, and he wonders if he can ask or if he should ask, if that is part of the reason he is here, and while he is wondering one of the caretakers wades back into the heap of things to get something else, because apparently something else is called for; whatever the caretaker has in mind is inside a cabinet, he has to move a baby carriage to open it and then he rummages inside it and he comes out with a raggedy doll and another clock. The first clock, the one already on the table, is an alarm clock with a pair of bells on the top and this other clock is more ornate, it would not look out of place on a mantelpiece or hanging on a wall, the one caretaker holds the clock and the doll up for the other caretaker to see and the other one, this is the one with whiskers, he nods his head and they put this other clock and the doll on the table too, and with that the caretakers look like they are satisfied. One of them claps the other on the shoulder and they turn to go, they push their cart out through the door—one of them walks backwards in front of the cart, to steer it, and the other pushes—and they leave Luca to do what he has come here to do.

He comes up to the table and he walks around it and he looks at what the caretakers have left for him—this class is a class for drawing still life, and what is on the table is what he is going to draw and he wonders how he is going to start. If there were a reason why he was drawing these particular things he could start with that, and he looks for a reason why the caretakers left these things for him and why they arranged them like this except that there might not be a reason, it might only be chance that they are arranged like this, and maybe that is why he did not ask them, because it would have been terribly disappointing if they had simply shrugged and had nothing to say. There is an easel here, waiting for him, and paper, pencils, and charcoal; he circles the table one more time then moves the easel so that when he stands at it he is looking at the table in a way that makes it make some kind of sense, and even if he could not say what that sense is it is still reassuring to feel like there is some kind of reason he is doing what he is doing. He settles into place and he draws, and when he starts to draw the light in the room is bright and full and slowly it empties, and his drawings get darker and darker and more solidly there on the paper before him; it is like the light draining away and the shadows that start to creep over them make what is in front of him real in a way the light alone did not. He does not notice as it happens, he is too immersed in what he is doing to realize it is happening and it is only after that he sees it—he is done and about to leave and he takes one look back, and that is when he sees how the drawings deepened and darkened as the day passed and it takes him a bit by surprise, to see what he had been doing all along. He leaves the drawings here, on the easel and scattered haphazardly around it, and later the caretakers will come for them and take them off to the gallery; they will come trundling back into the room with their cart between them, they will put the things on the table back in the cupboards and cabinets where they came from, they will wipe the top of the table with a dry cloth and then they will roll up Luca's drawings, carefully, so as not to smudge them, and they will stow them on their cart. But they will pause before they do, to look at them. They will wonder what would have happened if they had not moved the vase, what difference that would have made, and if it was right to have moved it—it is a tricky question and they will not work it out now but they will come closer, and eventually they will, perhaps the next time, with the next student, but not now. They will try again and Luca is going down a flight of stairs with one hand on the banister and his feet skipping from one step to the next, it is time for supper and he is on his way to the kitchens. In the great hall there is a class being taught, because sometimes a class will end up here, for one reason or another or for no reason at all, and if there is a reason it is usually to do with the light and if there is not it is usually the light as well, because of how satisfying it is to bask in it, and here is an instructor sitting at a table. It is the kind of table that would be in a café if it were not here; she sits at the table and there is a cup of tea in front of her, it sits in a saucer and she has a book in her hands, an old cloth-bound book with pages yellowing at the edges.

She sits and she reads and around her are students sitting on stools with pads of paper or sketchbooks, some of them are using easels but not all of them or even most of them, and they draw as the instructor sits and reads. Occasionally she will stop, and when she does she looks up into the distance; she does not look at anything in particular, she is only looking away from the book and she reaches a hand toward the cup of tea on the table without looking at it— she is still looking away into the distance, as if lost in thought, and she sips from the cup, returns it to its saucer and then goes back to her reading. This is one of the instructors. She teaches gestures, when she first came to the college that meant that she taught her students what it meant to draw a movement, how to preserve it in the stillness of a line, and for a while that was what she taught and how she taught but one day, when she was standing in front of a classroom, frozen in mid-stride—she had been demonstrating the moment of anticipation that happens in the body just before a step lands on the ground, how the anticipation slides into the step itself and how that is what walking is like—and she looked up and she saw her students drawing. This was not new, she had been watching students draw for years at this point, but this time when she looked up she saw something new, she saw that everything her students were doing was a gesture too, and how they were moving in response to her, even if they did not realize that that was what they were doing, and she was moving in response to them, in a kind of measured and meditative dance.

Now when she teaches, when her students sit around her to draw her reading, to draw what it is to be still and distracted by thoughts of something else that is somewhere else, as they start to get a feel for what that distance is like she ever so subtly changes the way that she is sitting—sometimes it is a change to the tilt of her head, sometimes it is how she is holding the book—whatever it is, it is to draw them further into what she is doing. She can feel them with her in the wide open contemplative space she has made, and she watches for how they try to make sense of it, of what it could look like, and when their pencils start to move more slowly, more evenly, she knows they have got it, and she takes a sip of her tea and Luca walks quietly past them, he crosses the hall and he carries on toward the kitchens. He comes down the stairs and he stretches himself up on his toes to look for Amalia, because it has been days since he last saw her and he does not see her, he sees Sasha instead and they say hello to one another, and the cooks have made pot pies for supper and they are serving them with a salad on the side and Luca would like to ask Sasha if he knows Amalia, and if he does then what he knows about her but he does not, because he is afraid he would blush if he did, and if he did he does not want to have to explain why, because that would mean blushing even more, so instead they talk about anything else. Sasha had a meeting with one of the professors and there is what they talked about, and Luca needed a new sketchbook and that was a trip out into the city yesterday, and Sasha is at ease with himself in a way that Luca is not, it makes Luca feel like there is too much of him when they are talking, like all of a sudden he does not know how to feel like he is not spilling out all over the place. Sasha is wearing a scarf looped loosely around his neck, because it is getting colder, and a shirt that is only a little more more buttoned up than the one he was wearing in the courtyard in the summer. Luca can see how his body moves as he goes between speaking and eating and listening and back again, and if only Luca did not feel so clumsy, if only he moved this easily, and when they have finished eating they take their plates back to the counter, they drop their forks and knives in the tray with all the other forks and knives and they leave, Sasha goes off one way and Luca is not sure where he is going to go.

He is not especially sure he wants to go back up to his room but it is where he goes, eventually—he wanders aimlessly up through the college for what feels like forever and then at last here it is, his door. He had been hoping he would not make it all the way here, he had been hoping something else would have happened. He had taken the most roundabout route he could think of to get here, past the secretary's office and then past the gallery, then over to where the workshops are and then gradually he looped his way back and now here he is, at his door, and he goes into his room and he closes the door behind him. He takes off his sweater, it is the one he was wearing when he saw Amalia, the one that is falling apart, he takes it off and he hangs it on a bedpost and he sits down on the bed. He does not feel right. He had been hoping that if something had happened, something that would have drawn him somewhere else than back up here, it would have helped, or at least it would have helped him to forget that his hair is a mess, which it usually is, of course, but now it is too much of a mess—it is greasy, it clumps on his head and it sticks to his skin, and he does not remember how long he has been wearing this t-shirt and it does not feel right against his skin either. He takes it off and he peels off his jeans and his socks and his underwear and somewhere in the room is a bathrobe and a towel, the towel is hanging on a hook on the back of the door and the bathrobe is somewhere under the bed, Luca has to kneel and stretch out an arm to reach it, and he slips it on and ties it closed, he goes out the door and down the stairs. Here is the door that would take him into the college and he goes past it, he keeps going down and here at the very bottom of the stairs, in the basement, is a washroom. The walls and the floor are tiled with small square ceramic tiles, there is someone brushing her teeth at one of the sinks and beyond the sinks are the baths, they are in little cubicles with swinging wooden doors and behind those doors are tubs sitting squatly on claw feet. Luca slips through one of the swinging doors and here is a tub and a ledge on the wall beside it, to put things like soap and shampoo and hairbrushes while having a bath, and he sits on the edge of the tub, he puts the plug in and he runs the water.

There is someone in the bath next to his, he can hear the water splashing as someone shifts in the tub on the other side of the wall and he sits on the edge of the tub here, he waits for it to fill and when it is full and there is steam rising from the water he slips out of his bathrobe, he steps into the bath with one foot and then the other and he lets himself sink into the water. The warmth of it seeps into his skin and into his body, and floating in it is almost like being held; he closes his eyes and he lets himself slip entirely under the water, so that for as long as he holds his breath there is only water and warmth, and it is like being safe, and secure, and when his breath runs out he comes up again with a small gasp. He sits up in the tub and he runs his hands through his hair and whatever this feeling is he feels better for it. He squeezes some shampoo into his hands, he scrubs his hair and then sinks back under the water to rinse it out, he half stands in the water to wash his body, and after all of that is done he sinks back into the water, to soak up every last bit of this warmth, and when it has run out he lets the water out of the tub and he runs the taps again, he rinses himself clean and he steps out. His skin prickles in the air and he reaches for his towel and he rubs himself dry, and when he is dry he pulls on his bathrobe again and goes out the swinging door.

Whoever was having a bath in the tub next to his has already gone, there is no one here but him and the tiles on the floor are cold under his feet; he hurries out of the washroom and back up the stairs and here is his room again. He had thought he had packed a comb but he cannot find it, he has looked in the backs of all his drawers and it is not there and it is not in his desk, it is not in the suitcase he brought with him and maybe he did not bring a comb with him after all. His hair is getting longer, it is what hair does, after all, and it is getting too long for him to just run his fingers through it, he should get a comb, or a brush, or he should have it cut, but that would be too much of a bother and he will likely get something like a brush instead, and when he has one he will try to remember to use it in the morning, when he gets up, but most days he will not or he will remember but he will not have the time to. For now he runs his fingers through his hair and that will do, and it has gotten late and he is not going to be awake for much longer, even though he wants to be—he never wants to go to bed and when he eventually does he never falls asleep easily, and then in the morning he has not slept enough and he cannot bear to wake up, but it is late, his eyes are too heavy and it feels like the whole rest of his body wants nothing more than for them to close even if he does not want them to, not yet, not quite yet. He goes over to the window and he stands up on his toes, he rests his arms on the windowsill and he looks out at the street below and the city stretching out around him, at the sky up above him and the stars he can only barely see past the lights of the city, but he looks for them anyway, like he would have before. He wonders what tonight would look like from there, if he were still there, and it is times like this he feels how far away he is, and the feeling does not make his heart twinge anymore. It did when he first got here, but not so much anymore, and even though the sprawling mess of this place still bewilders him and even if he does not yet understand how or what part he has to play here it is starting to feel like here is where he belongs. He smiles to himself and he steps away from the window, he turns the blankets back from the bed and he slips between the sheets, and when his head touches the pillow he is already drifting away into sleep.

When he wakes up he is lying on his stomach and his legs are sprawled out, the blankets are all tangled between them and the rest of him is bare. He rolls over and he sits up, he works his legs free from the blankets and he stands, or rather he totters, and he does what he can to work the sleep out of him, he searches the room for something to wear and after he has dressed he slips his sneakers on and he leaves. There is a lecture he is going to go to, it is for a class that he is fond of; it is taught by the professor who is his advisor, who he is supposed to go to see, to talk to, when there is something he needs to talk about, though most of the time when they meet it is just to talk about how all his classes are going, what he is learning and how he is doing. The first time they met she asked Luca how he was settling in and Luca was not sure how to answer, he had only just arrived, but they managed to talk about it anyway, or rather Luca rambled on about getting lost in the city and then lost in the college, and he tried to laugh about it but he was still afraid, back then, though he never would have said he was, and the professor sat across from him, in her armchair, and she nodded when he needed someone to nod and she listened, and that alone would be enough for him to like this class but he also likes it anyway. He likes that it is not a class about some very specific thing, like the history of pencil-making or still life, or how to make paints, it is a course on general methodology, and though that may sound hopelessly obtuse, the way that this professor teaches makes it into something beautiful. When the class starts and the professor starts to speak they start somewhere, with something, of course, but the professor steps back from it, she shows where it is and how it fits where it is, how it has a purpose, and when she speaks in her quiet voice Luca gets a sense of how very large the world is and how he could fit into it.

He is still in a corridor somewhere, on his way there, and he does not expect to see Mattie, because Mattie is not in this class, she is much more interested in the history of pencil-making and that class is at the same time as this class, but he sees her—they are going in opposite directions and they stop, they say, hello; behind her glasses there are clumps of mascara in her eyelashes, because she has taken to wearing mascara, even though she has not quite figured out how it goes on, and Luca's hair is standing up in ways it probably should not be because it was still wet when he fell asleep last night, and that is what life is like these days. They are buried so deep in what they are doing that there is barely any time left for anything else, it is just one thing after another and it is exhilarating to have this much to do, and also they are glad to see one another; even if there is no time, even if they cannot stop for long, it is still good to see one another, to be reminded of everything they would say if they did still have the time—how they are settling in here, how being this busy is a kind of settling in, how it is a life starting to take shape around them and if only there were more time. They will get together soon, they say, they will tell one another everything then and it does not really matter if they do so long as they both know that they would, and they say goodbye and they carry on to where they were going.

Mattie is on her way to her class and the lecture Luca is going to is in one of the studios, it is not one of the studios Luca has worked in but it is the same kind of white room with a high ceiling and stuff heaped all along the walls, and there are things to sit on set out—there are chairs and a bench and other things like crates and coffee tables that probably should not be sat on but they will do for now, and in front of them all is a lectern, and here is the professor already standing at it. She is wrapped in sweaters and scarves and long cardigans, and somewhere in all that flowing cloth she is small in a way that only old people are small. Her shoulders stoop and her wrists are too thin, there is too much bone to them, her hair is grey and lines have riddled the skin around her eyes. Her fingers play with the cuffs of one of her cardigans, not nervously, it is what she does when she is thinking, and her hair would float in wisps like her scarves do if it were not gathered up and sitting in a bun at the nape of her neck. Luca comes in and he finds a place to sit, and the professor's eyes flicker toward him and she smiles, briefly, because she knows him; her smile is always only a flicker, it lasts only long enough for Luca to think that he sees it and then she looks away again.

She looks away because she always looks away, to somewhere else, or it would be if there really was somewhere she is looking away to. There is a weariness in this old woman's eyes, it is a sadness that has always been with her, for as long as she can remember it has weighed on her, when she is doing well it reminds her of how much worse it could be and when she is not doing well it is a pit; it has made her guarded, and too careful, there are too many things she has not done for fear of the risk, and things she has done anyway that left her feeling broken after. She has had to learn to navigate all this, and she has, and it has made her stronger, and wiser, and weary—she is always weary, and it is not just because of her age—and when she looks away it is to keep all this hidden away. It is not what she wants to teach, it is not what she wants for her students. They will all know sadness, it will come to them all eventually but for some of them not yet, and that is what matters, not yet. These lives can carry on a little longer without knowing the weight of it, and so she smiles briefly, fleetingly, she hopes for the best for them and she looks away. She runs a finger along the edge of the lectern, it is how she gathers herself together, it is how she readies herself to speak, and when she speaks her eyes follow the line her finger has made across the lectern, like she is reading from it, and it is little more than a whisper, her voice, it carries only far enough to be heard, like a secret entrusted only to those here—because Luca is of course not the only one here, even though sitting on his rickety wooden chair near to the door and craning forward to hear, it feels like he is. In front of him, on a simple bench, two boys sit close together, and a girl sits beside them and in front of them are other students sitting on other sorts of things, and they all sit, raptly, and then when the lecture is over everyone stands up from where they were sitting and listening and they are still quiet, as if there is still something to listen to lingering in the air, some way to keep themselves caught up in the world the professor had laid out for them, and when they leave the professor is still at the front of the room. She looks smaller now, her eyes droop and she is leaning her weight against the lectern, and soon the caretakers will come to take it away. They will help her to a seat and she will rest while they put away the various stools and benches and chairs they set out for the lecture, all of them except for the one the professor is resting on, and when they are done they will leave, and she will stay a while longer, in the quiet of the empty room, to rest a little longer, and then she too will leave, making her way, slowly and secretly, to some other part of the college, and Luca is on his way down to the kitchens, to eat; it is nearly time for supper and he winds his way down to the kitchens to eat; he winds through the college without thinking about where he is going or how to get there, he knows the way now, he knows the college and it leads him to the kitchens and Amalia is already here and at last, Luca has found her. She is sitting at a table with her supper in front of her, she is just starting to eat and Luca's stomach does a little dance to see her again, he tries to wave to her but she does not see him, or at least Luca does not think she has seen him; she is sitting by herself, there are empty places to either side of her and if he hurries, if he can get his supper before Amalia finishes hers and if no one else sits beside her then Luca could sit next to her, and so he gets a plate and he grabs for the cutlery and he keeps looking back to where Amalia is, as if it would make a difference, and he does not think Amalia has seen him but he is not sure. He hopes she has not, because what if she did see him and what if she thought nothing of it and he holds out his plate and a cook puts a ladleful of pasta on it, and a cream sauce of some kind, with mushrooms in it, and Amalia did not leave while Luca's back was turned. Luca was worried she would but she did not, she has not finished eating and Luca sits down next to her, he sits down and he puts his plate down in front of him, and his fork, and he would have put his knife down too but he does not have a knife, he did not think to get one, he did not think he would need one, and he hopes he will not because it would be embarrassing to need one and not have thought to get one and he stops, worrying about it will not change anything, he takes a breath, he turns toward Amalia and he says, hello, and Amalia says hello and they have said hello again, they are sitting next to one another again. They sit and they eat, or they almost do—they have their suppers in front of them and occasionally one or the other of them remembers to take a bite but mostly there are things to say, and questions to be asked, questions to do with all the time since the last time they saw one another, and then questions about all the time before that, and they ask and they answer breathlessly, and with every answer there is more to ask and of course there is not enough time for all this, no matter how slowly they eat, and when they have finally eaten the last of what is on their plates they are nearly alone here. The cooks are gathering up the last of the dishes, there is someone in a corner lost in a book, the caretakers have come down for their suppers and then to have a drink with the head cook. Amalia composes herself, she has gotten carried away and forgot herself and she gathers her hands in her lap and she asks, what are you doing now, and Luca does not know, and Amalia says, come out with me.

It is getting colder and colder outside and so they cannot just go, they must go back to their rooms for jackets or sweaters and maybe even scarves or hats; they agree that they will go and get their things and then they will meet in the great hall, at the foot of the stairs, and then they will go out. They nod their heads and they are about to go up to their rooms but they stand there a moment longer, before they do, they cannot help it, and then they pull away from one another and Amalia goes up into the college one way and Luca goes another. He almost runs through the corridors, then up a flight of stairs and through another door and here are the stairs going up to his room, and when he gets to his door he is out of breath and his jacket should be hanging on the back of the door, there is a hook for it there, next to the hook his towel is hanging from, and it is not, he finds it draped over the back of the chair instead. He grabs it and he grabs a sweater from the floor, because his jacket is an old jean jacket and it is not especially warm, he goes back down the stairs and he pulls his sweater over his head as he goes, it has a hood and a pocket in the front for his hands and the sleeves are too long, sometimes he rolls them up but mostly he does not, there are holes in the cuffs and he likes how his thumbs can fit through them, and Amalia's coat buttons up the front and it has a belt that cinches around her waist and she is already here when Luca arrives back in the great hall; she is standing with her hands in the pockets of her coat and Luca raced some of the way and then not the rest, so he would not be out of breath when he arrived and when he arrives he is slightly out of breath anyway, and Amalia's cheeks are slightly flushed, as if she is slightly out of breath too, and together they leave the college. One after another they go down the lane, they tumble out into the street and Amalia knows a bar nearby, it's this way, she says, and she takes Luca's hand and Luca follows, he has no idea where they could possibly be going and he follows. They go down the street and down another and it is dark enough out that the darkness has a weight to it—the street lights have come on, to try to keep it from weighing too heavily, and because it is nearly winter, when the nights are especially heavy there are garlands of lights strung between them, draped from one streetlight to the next all down the street, and they are glad they went back for their jackets, there is a biting chill to the air and the garlands of lights twinkle above them like the stars they cannot see overhead.

Amalia's hair trails freely behind her and she leads them through the streets, and the city lights up around them as the day comes to its end and the night starts to stir and here they are, they have arrived, here is the bar Amalia knows. If it were still warmer out there would be tables set out in front and people sitting with drinks in hand but it is not, there is only an awning overhead and the open space where those tables would go if they were not stacked off to one side against the wall, and the door is a plain and unremarkable door, Amalia pushes to open it and the two of them go through and inside it is dark, or it is almost dark—there are lights set into the walls, and booths to sit in under them, and in the middle of the room is a chandelier that blossoms into slivers of fluted glass and lights nested in them and glittering. There is a gentle murmur of people talking and music playing somewhere, and waitresses and waiters sweeping from one table to another and when they come in through the door Luca stops, agape. The wood of the walls is scuffed and scratched, the tables and chairs were all dragged in from wherever they were found and the chandelier is slowly falling to pieces and all of it is beautiful, he wants to say, but Amalia takes his hand and she leads them to a table, Amalia sits on one side of it and Luca on the other and the seats of the chairs are soft and velvety and probably red, Luca cannot quite tell, but they are stained and torn and patched and a waiter comes, wearing a white shirt with stains on the cuffs and a bow tie, and he says, good evening, he asks if they would care for anything and yes, they would please. The waiter nods and slips away and there is a candle on the table between them, it sits flickering in a glass cup and it is just enough to light up their faces and leave the shadows thick around them.

Their waiter brings them a carafe of wine, he places it on the table between them and then come a pair of glasses, he fills them with a flourish then slips away to the next table, to ask the people sitting there if they would care for anything. This is one of Amalia's favourite places, it is a place she comes to when she feels too adrift or alone and needs to be somewhere familiar, somewhere that will feel like home even if it is not. She is not from here either, she does not speak much of where she is from or what her family is like; it feels like she does not want to and Luca understands that, so he does not ask, but he does know that she came from somewhere else too. Most of the students at the college did, and those that did not, those who came from somewhere in the city, they left their homes too. And all of them had a reason to, some nagging sense that they might not ever be able to put into words that they just do not belong. The college is a place for people who will not ever belong anywhere, this is what Amalia thinks, it is a place that offers that sort of person a strange kind of hope. And this bar is another. She raises her glass and they drink, and all along the walls in the other booths there are people gathered, here where they can sit among themselves without any sort of worry. Later there will be dancing, some nights there is a band up on the stage where there is only a single music stand now, other nights the music plays itself and everyone comes out onto the floor dressed in their finest. They are a ragtag and mismatched bunch, because everyone who comes here has their own idea of what finery is—there are second-hand dresses and bow ties crookedly tied and here and there a glimpse of fishnets or a ratty old pair of sneakers and all of it is jumbled together, sometimes all on the same person. Luca and Amalia have nearly finished their wine and the waiter has reappeared at the foot of the table, he reaches for the empty carafe and he does not say anything, there is no need, he raises an eyebrow and that is enough to ask if they would like another and yes, of course. The night is well under way now, the lights in the chandelier are turned down so low they may as well not be on, the candle between Luca and Amalia flickers and they cannot really see anything of whatever is happening beyond it. The second carafe does not last long; they laugh their way through it and when it is done they sit back, they are quite drunk and around them the bar has filled, soon it will spill over and the dancing will begin and Amalia sits back and she tilts her head, her smile is open and unguarded and she asks, whatever will we do with ourselves next.

―

When they eventually end up leaving they come stumbling out of the bar and into the street—it is later, it is much, much later and they are sweating from dancing and still very drunk and they look one way and then the other and they go this way, down what they hope is the street they came along. The street lights over their heads are still lit even though the sky is starting to lighten and they stumble along close together, and sometimes when they stumble they topple together, and once when they do Amalia slips her hand into the crook of Luca's arm, she draws him closer and she rests her head on his shoulder. They are in the lane now, somehow they have managed to find their way back, and there are no street lights here, only the occasional light bleeding out from a window looking out into the lane and the sliver of very nearly blue sky up above them, winding its way ever closer to the college. They will be back soon, and when they get back this night will have ended and everything else that is life will start up again and so they are quiet, because if they are quiet then this last part of it will last longer. They are so close together Luca can feel the warmth rising from this girl's body, he soaks it up, as much of it as he can, and when they come to the great hall they do not say goodbye, they stop as if they are going to and then they do not, they turn and they face one another and they do not say anything, Amalia takes Luca's hand in hers and she leads him up the stairs.

Luca does not know where they are, he has not ever come this way before, he has not ever had a reason to; he thinks they are near the library but he is not sure, he is too tired and still too drunk to be sure and they go past what might have been the library and here is a way up to what was once an attic and up here the ceiling slopes, by the door it is as high as a ceiling ought to be and on the opposite wall it is not, and there is a neatly made bed and next to it is a desk, with books arranged precisely on it, and a closet next to the desk. They come in through the door and Amalia closes it behind them and they are standing in the almost dark, and then there is a lamp casting a soft glow into the room. Amalia takes off her jacket and her shoes and Luca slips his sneakers off, one and then the other, and Amalia sits down on one side of the bed. There is enough room for Luca to sit beside her and he hesitates a moment, he is still standing by the door, he does not know that he does not have to hesitate, and then he has taken a deep breath and come to the bed. He is sitting beside Amalia. It is a small bed and they are close enough together for their legs to touch and Amalia knows what will happen, and she waits, she waits for Luca to raise a hand to touch her hair with just the tips of his fingers, she waits while Luca searches her eyes, to see if what he has done is right. Amalia's eyes are dark, and in the dark they are bottomless and inscrutable, and when Luca moves his hand to touch her cheek Amalia lowers her eyes and her lips part, she guides Luca's hand to her mouth and gently she kisses the tips of the trembling boy's fingers.

When Luca wakes up he is lying with his head nestled in the crook of Amalia's shoulder, he is wearing only his t-shirt and his underpants, and Amalia is wearing only a slip, because she is of course the sort of girl who would wear a slip under a dress; sometime in the night she held her hair up and Luca searched with his fingers up and down her back for the buttons keeping her dress done up, one by one he fumbled them open and the dress fell away and Amalia's body is soft, her skin smells of soap or a delicate perfume and Luca lies with his cheek on her skin and his arm around her and their legs tangled together and Amalia stirs beneath him as she wakes up too, and now that they are awake Luca untangles his arms and Amalia slides out from under him and they lie so that they can see one another. Amalia runs a finger along the collar of Luca's t-shirt and they steal glances at one another, and sometimes their eyes meet, and when they do a nervous feeling leaps in them. It is almost too much to bear and all the more exciting for it, and there is a window above them, sunlight washes over them and they are naked—even if they are only almost naked they feel entirely naked and tender and too aware of every time their skin touches. Amalia's fingertips explore Luca's collarbones and then they go further under his shirt and Luca takes in the whole expanse of Amalia's body, her skin, her breath rising and falling under her slip, her legs curled against his and they have to get up, they have to get out of bed and somehow, eventually, they do. Luca picks his jeans up from where they fell and Amalia picks out a dress to wear and they stumble one after another down the stairs and toward the kitchens, they are clumsy enough to make them wonder if they are maybe still a little drunk, and in the kitchens breakfast is well under way.

The tables are filling and the cooks are scurrying back and forth between the stoves and there are other students waiting in line for their breakfasts; Luca and Amalia are ragged at the edges, they are still sleepy and dishevelled and as the drunkenness drains from them they start to realize just how tired they are. Amalia steps closer to Luca and she rests her head on his shoulder, she asks, how much longer, and when they arrive at the front of the line the cooks take one look at them and are sure to pick out the biggest mugs they can find for their coffees, they serve them plates of scrambled eggs with fried tomatoes and toast to the side, and the two of them take their plates and they go off to one of the far corners of the kitchens, where it is a little quieter—it is not quiet, there is nowhere here that is quiet, if the cooks are not clattering about then there are the other students talking, or laughing, but here it is quieter and they sit together, and first they sip quietly at their coffees and then when they have drunk enough of it that they are feeling more properly awake they remember. Luca wonders what has happened, and what it means, and he does not know what will happen next and he does not ask, he is too afraid to ask, it is enough that Amalia seems to know what she is doing and so they sit close together, so that they are touching, and it feels like this is how they should be sitting and Luca wants to stay like this except that he has a class he has to go to. He starts to stand up to go and he almost stands and then he reaches for Amalia instead, and Amalia draws him close and they press together and this time Luca does not worry about holding her too tight. He wraps his arms around her and he buries his face in her hair, and Amalia's breath is warm on his neck and they hold one another for what seems like forever and then, when he eventually leaves the kitchens, he goes up the stairs slowly, one step at a time, because there is only so much that a cup of coffee can do, he wobbles across the great hall and he vanishes into the college.

His feet drag through the corridors and he leans on the banister as he climbs the stairs, his head is starting to ache, it will only get worse as the day goes on and he wonders how he is going to get through it. He comes to the top of a flight of stairs and then he has to climb another and here is a studio, it may be a studio he has been in before or it may not be—there are any number of studios in the college, all with the same white walls and windows and piles of stuff along the walls, and their ceilings too high overhead, and it is always like coming back to the same room, even though he is usually in a completely different part of the college, it always feels like coming back to the same place. He comes in the door and this time around easels have been set up all around the room, all facing the middle of it, and here in the middle of it is a table. It is not a table to sit at, it is a table to sit around, it would be in its proper place with a sofa to one side of it and a pair of armchairs to the other and a tea set, with a pot and cups set out and there is no sign of any of that, instead there is a course cloth draped over it, to keep the surface from getting too scuffed, an instructor standing on top of it, and students standing at most of the easels. Some of them are already drawing the instructor and how he is standing, some are still getting ready and still others have not yet arrived. There are still easels with no one standing at them, and when Luca comes into the room he goes to one of those and there are sheets of paper already set out and waiting for him, he slips into place and he fumbles with the paper, as if he is getting ready to draw but really he is hoping that if he takes his time it will be enough for the thickness to work its way out from behind his eyes but it is not, his head is still as heavy as it was. The instructor standing on the table is barefoot and he is standing with his arms at his sides, as if he were standing somewhere else, somewhere where there were not people gathered around him and looking up at him. The door creaked when Luca came in and the instructor had half turned his head toward the sound, and now that Luca has taken his place the instructor turns as if to look out the windows, as if he were alone here and slightly bored, as if there might be something out there to see.

The windows here look out over a lane, it is too narrow and they are too far up to see it but somewhere down there is a lane, and the college is on one side of it and on the other side are other buildings, and the windows of those buildings might look into the backs of workshops or offices of some kind or another, or they could be where people live, and the instructor stands as if he is looking out the window, toward these other windows, except that he is not. He is not looking at anything, he is simply here. His hands are open and there is no feeling flickering across his face, he is calm and he stands here as himself and not anything else, and later there will be classes where he is doing something else, or another of the instructors doing something else, but not yet. First it is important to learn what a person is when they are not anything else and so he stands, so the students can see his limbs and what it is for limbs to be, how his neck rises from his spine, how a body can simply and completely exist. Because it is important to remember that no matter what else there is, there is this. There is always this.

Luca picks out a pencil and he lifts it to the paper and his hand wobbles from how groggy he still is; he looks up to where the instructor is standing and it takes a moment for his eyes to settle on him, and then another to make the first line on the paper and the line is too thick, too heavy, his hand is not light like it should be and he draws anyway, without being at all sure of what he is doing. He looks back and forth between the instructor and the paper and here is how he is feeling taking form before him—it is in the clumsiness and the uncertainty of the lines he makes, how he is tired, but it is more than how he is tired. It is how something has changed and everything has changed, how he does not know what will happen next or even what to do now and if he does not know that then how could he possibly draw. He wants to, he wants to stretch out into this, into what is happening, whatever it is, no matter that it makes him foolish or clumsy, he wants what is happening to happen and he draws, and when the class is over the instructor steps down from the table, first one foot and then the other, and Luca looks at what he has drawn and he has made a mess of what he was supposed to do or he has done it perfectly, he cannot tell. The caretakers have come in, wheeling their cart ahead of them, and the other students step away from their easels and talk with one another while they get ready to leave and the caretakers gather up all the various drawings from the various easels and Luca does not join the others, he does not want to talk, not this morning; instead he wanders over to the windows and he looks outside, at the buildings across from him, at the windows here and there on the walls facing him and they are not part of the school, they look out from rooms that have nothing at all to do with what is happening here. He cannot quite see into them—they are too far or too small or the sun is reflecting on the glass, and he wonders what could be happening in them. It is still early in the morning and here is a man who has just woken up, he is standing in his bathroom with lather on his face and he is slowly and methodically dragging a razor through it, here is a woman sitting on the edge of her bed, she has just come from her bathroom and her hair is wet; she leans forward, so it falls over her shoulder and she brushes it out in long, even strokes and here is an office where everyone is already getting ready for the day to start, the first of the clerks has arrived and a pot of coffee is almost ready, and the clerk is looking out the window and waiting for it to finish, with the same faraway look that the instructor had when he was almost looking out the window, and Luca cannot see any of this, he can only imagine what life is like in the rest of this city and he wants to be a part of that, too, and the caretakers come to his easel, they take his drawings from off his easel and they stow them on the trolley with all the others. Everyone else has already left—the instructor slipped his shoes back on and he left, and the other students drifted out after him, one after another, and Luca has not, not yet. He stays at the window, looking out, looking up at the sky, and he wonders what is out there and what it is and what it is like. He remembers that he is tired, and why, and he could topple so easily into sleep but not yet, please not yet. It does not matter how tired he is or how tired he will be, he wants to see Amalia again, and then again, and he hopes he will find her, without knowing precisely how to, or what will happen when he eventually does. Everything that has happened and what he is feeling is bewildering, and he does not entirely understand any of it but that is okay, so long as it does not stop and he need not worry, Amalia will find him again. It will be in a corridor, as she is coming out of the library, or she will appear behind him in the kitchens; she will touch his shoulder and he will turn and look up, he will see Amalia and Amalia will say, hello, and there will be a question in her voice, and Luca will reach for her, and Amalia will smile, she will come closer to him and lift his head up, to kiss him.

It gets colder and colder at night, and then the winter comes; snow falls and turns the streets to slush, coats are taken out from the backs of the closets where they have been since the last of the snow melted away last year, the streets turn to a shuffle of scarves and hands thrust deep into pockets and then it starts to warm again. It is almost enough to open the windows at night again and so Luca opens his, even if it is only almost warm enough to be opening up the windows at night. He cannot help it, the fresh air is too much of a relief from the stagnant weight of winter, he opens it a crack before he goes to bed and when he wakes up he kicks the blankets off, he sits up and his skin prickles against the chill in the air. He pulls on a t-shirt and his jeans and he picks up a sweater from the floor, because it is still a little too cold to get away with not wearing a sweater, he takes a moment to try to get his hair to lie flat and either he has forgotten about socks or he has decided against them, he slips his shoes on his bare feet and he leaves. It is later than it should be but if he is lucky then he may still be in time to get something for breakfast and so he is on his way down to the kitchens, and if Amalia is still there, in the kitchens, then they will sit together—if they are both there then they will always be sitting together and sometimes there are others with them, sometimes it is Mattie and sometimes Sasha and sometimes someone else entirely and sometimes it is only them, and if it is only them they sit too close together and very nearly disappear into one another, and somehow they remember they have classes to go to and somehow they leave before it is too late. And if Amalia is not in the kitchens then she has probably already eaten and left, because Luca is not nearly as good at getting up in the morning as she is, and he comes down to the kitchens late and he eats and after he has eaten, before he goes off to wherever it is he is off to that day, he passes by the library. He slips through the door and into the seat beside Amalia, if Amalia is here. He nuzzles close to her and she looks up from whatever she was just reading and she kisses him, and sometimes there are things to say and other times Luca will just sit quietly beside her for a couple of minutes and sometimes Amalia is not here at all, and when Luca comes through the door the librarian looks up from her desk, she straightens her glasses, she sees Luca and she shakes her head with the sort of smile all librarians have—it is a discrete and knowing smile that can be trusted to keep nearly any secret safe. The librarian smiles and Luca grins lopsidedly and he leaves, and then there are lectures or time spent alone in a studio somewhere, working on something, and later Luca will find Amalia, or Amalia will find Luca, and they will vanish into the depths of the college together. Where they go only they know, though the caretakers will find out, eventually, when they open up a room they thought had been locked only to find traces of someone who had been there before them—they will find footsteps all through the dust, or a window that was opened and not closed entirely after, and a curtain rustling in the breeze, and while they tidy up and put things back in their proper places they will wonder who it might have been who was here, out of curiosity more than anything else.

Later, when the two of them are tired, they stumble up to one of their rooms, sometimes they go to Luca's and sometimes they go to Amalia's, they come in through the door and somehow they remember to close it behind them and they are already pressed together, their mouths searching and their hands wrestling with whatever they happen to be wearing. They topple into bed and in the morning they wake up slowly, they linger together until eventually they absolutely have to be up, and Luca pulls on his jeans and helps Amalia to button her dress, because he likes to help button her dresses up as much as he likes to unbutton them, and when they leave Luca has sort of brushed his hair but only just barely. It is still mussed and slept on, and when they have sat down in the kitchens for breakfast one of them usually has to fix it. They arrive in the kitchens together and the cooks have made scrambled eggs with oregano and slivers of green onion and slices of toast to the side, the smell of it drifts up the stairs to greet them and they pick up a pair of plates from where there are plates waiting for them and they get in line to wait to be served. They are quiet this morning, it is nearly the end of the year and they are distracted by all the things that come at the end of the year—Amalia has papers to write and Luca has the end of year show to prepare for, and they eat quickly without saying much of anything and when they have eaten all they are going to eat Amalia takes one last sip of her tea and then they leave, they go upstairs together and they whisper goodbye in a corner of the great hall, Amalia goes off to the library and Luca goes up the stairs and through the double doors to the gallery. The end of year show will be here, when it happens, and Luca's work is already here, waiting for him; most of it is in this cabinet and the rest of it is on the two shelves next to it, and out in the gallery proper is the space where he will show his work when the time comes to show it. There are other students already here and there, moving between the back, where their work has been kept, and where they will be showing it—Mattie is here, kneeling in front of the stretch of wall where her work will go. She has not put anything up yet, it is all arranged in neat piles in front of her and she picks up a drawing and she holds it in her hands, she looks up at the wall and then down at her hands and the sheet of paper held between them. All her work is small and finely detailed, it has to be looked at very closely and she is trying to figure out how she is going to use a wall when everything she has made should be held close, in the hands. Luca opens the cabinet where his drawings are, and inside there are drawers that slide out and he slides a drawer out and here are a pair of drawings, he takes them out, one after another, and then he opens the next one and the next one, he takes all his drawings out and bundles them together, and he goes to his stretch of wall and it is his turn to wonder how to arrange them.

When it is done—and it is done, eventually, for a while it did not feel like it would ever be done but everything is ready, or it is close enough, it is done, and the gallery is ready to open for the show. Luca has not yet gone in, he is still standing out in the great hall—he has come fresh from the bath, he has washed his hair and brushed it thoroughly and he hopes it stays in place without being at all sure that it will. He is wearing a suit, and it has been ages since he last wore a suit, if he ever has, he did not even have one, he did not think he would need one here and he and Amalia had to go out into the city to a shop that sold all sorts of suits and fancy dresses to find one he could wear. It looked like it would be a small shop but it was anything but, it only looked small from the street but inside it turned out to be a very long and narrow shop, and stretching the whole length of it there were racks with dresses hanging on them on one side and suits on the other. There were more kinds of suits there than Luca had ever seen before and with every suit they pulled from the racks they wondered what sort of a person would have worn it, because every one of these suits had been worn before making its way here; they looked for clues and they made up stories about who those people might have been and the suit they eventually found for him is simple and grey, a light grey with broad lapels and he is wearing a white shirt with it but not a tie, because if he was not sure about wearing a suit then he was less sure about a tie, and even though they looked they could not find one that he liked enough. He is standing at the top of the stairs, just outside the doors to the gallery; the doors are open and there are people already inside but he stays where he is because he is waiting for Amalia, and when she arrives she comes up the stairs wearing one of the dresses that she only takes out for special occasions, when she wants to be dressed especially nicely. It is silk and trimmed with brocade that floats lightly around her, her hair is gathered up and pinned neatly into place and she comes to the top of the stairs and she says, hello Luca, and Luca says, hello Amalia, she takes Luca's hand and together they go inside.

Inside there are platters of little things to eat—different kinds of fruit cut up and neatly arranged and melted chocolate to dip it in, crackers with slices of cheese or thin slivers of salmon placed on the tops of them, tiny cakes with swirls of chocolate inside—and the cooks are all here, except tonight they are not cooks, instead of their kitchen whites they are wearing jackets and black ties and they will be the waiters for the event; they have arranged the platters of food on a table in the middle of the room, and they come in with fresh platters whenever one starts to look a little empty, the head cook is standing at the head of the table, wearing an overflowing dress and pouring drinks, she hands them to whoever happens to be near enough to take one, and if there is no one nearby then she is always good for another glass herself and even the principal is here, she has come down from her apartment for the occasion. She strides into the room with a long tweed skirt trailing behind her, and a jacket and a broach at her throat to hold the collar of her shirt in place; her hair is thick, and dark, and shot through with grey, and it would be very long if it was not gathered into a thick braid and then pinned up into a bun crowning her head. Her hands are clasped behind her back and she is tall, she towers over everyone else here, and partly it is because she actually is tall and the rest of it is how the whole entire room and everyone in it falls into place around her. She looks out over it all with a calm, unknowable gaze and this is the first time Luca has seen her. He has heard about her, of course, she is whispered about endlessly among the students, as if she were a myth or a legend. Everyone falls quiet around her as she walks slowly around the room; she goes from one student's work to the next, her eyes pass over the drawings and paintings and sculpted and woven things and she nods, and occasionally she will pause to look more closely at something—the brushwork of a painting, or how the light falls on a particular sculpture, and later, after she has gone all the way around the gallery and taken in the entire show, she will have words to say to everyone. She will stand in the middle of the room and the secretary will tap the side of a glass with a knife, everyone will fall quiet at the sound and that will be the moment the year ends, but it has not happened yet. The head cook has had to call for more wine and Luca's drawings are here, on this wall by the door, the principal has not yet made her way this far around the gallery and Luca and Amalia are standing here, waiting for her to come. They have glasses of wine and a plate of grapes to share between the two of them and they pick at the grapes and they wait, and while they are waiting they empty their glasses and they go back for more, and for a slice of a raspberry cheesecake that has just come up from the kitchen, and while a cook is lifting their slice of cake onto a plate the principal comes to where Luca's work is. She bends to look more closely at a drawing of a little boy who would not sit still while Luca was drawing, so that he had started to draw him one way and he moved and Luca ended up with something else, and Luca liked how the drawing changes in the middle, how there is a movement in it that makes something impossible out of his body, and the principal straightens again, and she may have smiled when she figured out what had happened but Luca cannot tell what that means, and then the principal has moved on, and then she has made her way all around the gallery, she has seen everything and she has come to the middle of the gallery to say what she has to say—everyone else falls quiet and when she speaks it is in a deep, clear voice that fills the room, and when she has finished then the evening is over.

The cooks have come to clear the room of half-eaten platters and glasses and bottles, and there are still some people lingering in the gallery and others who have spilled out into the great hall, because even if the year is over no one is ready for everything to be over, and there are plans forming for where to go and what to do next. Luca and Amalia have already slipped away back into the college, they are winding through it and somewhere behind them there are people trickling away into the city and the night, in search of a bar and more to drink and Luca and Amalia stumble through corridor after corridor and as they go a quiet settles around them; the college is emptying out and they feel very nearly alone, and in the quiet it is like their clothes are unravelling or melting away. They tumble together, they cannot help themselves, they want to too badly and too much, they tumble together and their hands reach and their mouths open, their breath comes heavily and their mouths come together and then they are moving again, hand in hand and gasping. At the beginning of the night Amalia had gathered all her hair up and tied it back with a clip and it hung neatly down her back and now it drapes thickly around her and her dress has slipped from her shoulders, sweat makes it cling to her skin and it tangles around her belly and her hips and the buttons on Luca's shirt are very nearly all undone and they come through a door and here is Amalia's room. They grab hold of one another, they grope at the clasps and buttons and belts barely keeping them clothed and then they are not, their clothes have fallen entirely away and Amalia is wearing nylons and they have to stop, they have to try to figure out the problem of getting them off her when they are both this drunk and this is it, the year is over—their legs twine together and they hold onto one another and it might be dark but their eyes are bright, and fierce, and there is a hunger to how they burrow together into the tangle of their bodies together in this bed, and if only they could have their fill, if only it were possible, if only the year was not over.

Even when the dark starts to lift from around them they do

not let go, they do not stop, their breath runs ragged and sore and when morning breaks they are lying naked and pressed together, their legs knotted, their skin soft with sweat, their breath rising and falling inside an exhausted and uneasy sleep.

The Summer

*L*uca wakes up and he is in a different bed. It is bigger than his bed at the college and it sags in the middle, when he sleeps he sinks into it and he has dreams of being trapped or smothered or drowned. It is the summer, and he sleeps without blankets, he has only a sheet between him and the night and when he wakes up he is sticky with sweat, he has to peel the sheet from his body and the air against his skin is a relief. He peels the sheet away and he lies there, on his back, and the air moves over his skin and he does not especially want to get up but he does. He lets out a breath that is almost a sigh, he takes a deep breath in and then another and then he gets out of the bed. It is never easy, getting out out of this bed, he has to reach out and pull himself out of the sunken bit in the middle of it. It is a little like climbing, and then he is sitting on the edge of the mattress, where it is still firm. He sleeps wearing nothing or next to nothing because it is not possible to sleep any other way and he stands, he tries to stretch himself out, he tries to work out the kinks in his neck and his back that he always gets from sleeping in this bed.

There is a window in the room and the window is open, and a door that is also open, and between them a fan is standing and turning from left to right and then back again and still it is too hot to sleep. He goes out the door and he is in the middle of a hallway, at one end of it is the door to the stairs that lead to the street, and across from him is the door to the bathroom and the door to the other bedroom, and at the other end of it is the kitchen. He is in an apartment over a shop on a street not far from the college. It is summer and the college is closed, he could not stay there and so he is spending the summer here. He goes to the kitchen and there is a kettle on the stove, he takes it and he fills it from the tap, he yawns while the water runs and when it is full enough he puts it back on the stove to boil. Mattie has already left for work. She left the dishes from her breakfast on the table and while Luca waits for the kettle to boil he puts them in the sink with the rest of the dirty dishes. The kettle is simmering but not yet boiling and he goes back to his room. He is wearing only his underpants and he should get dressed. There is a dresser against one of the walls but he is not using it; his clothes are all in the backpack he brought with him, or on the floor next to it. He fishes a shirt from the pile next to it and he puts it on, he does up some of the buttons and it is too hot to be wearing much of anything else so he does not.

He goes back to the kitchen and the kettle has boiled, it is whistling on the stove and he takes a mug from beside the sink and he looks in a cupboard for a tea bag and he does not find one, the jar with all the tea bags in it is already out on the counter, from when Mattie made herself a cup of tea. He closes the cupboard and he takes a tea bag and he drops it into a mug, he takes the kettle from the stove and he fills it. There is a balcony behind the kitchen, and a fire escape going down from it to the alley—it is where they have to take their garbage to be picked up—and sitting on the balcony are a pair of chairs Mattie found in the next alley over. She found them on her way home one night, she came home and then she and Luca went back out to get them. Someone had thrown them out and they brought them up here instead and now they have somewhere to sit. Luca sits with his mug and he puts his feet up on the railing and he waits for his tea to steep, and if Mattie were here she would be sitting beside him and she would have a cup of tea too. They would wait together while their tea steeped and then had cooled enough to drink. In between sips they would talk, and it would not have the urgency or intensity of the way that they talked when they first met one another. They are not as lost as they were then. They have found places here where they fit, and now when they talk it is about what is happening here. Almost everyone from the college has gone back to wherever they live when they are not at the college. Mattie stayed for the summer because she wanted to learn to make paper, there is a mill in the city where it is still made by hand and she has found a job there. It is hard work but she likes it. She likes how she has to use her hands, how she has to feel the paper to make it, and even if she comes home every evening aching it is worth it. Sasha had said he was going to stay for the summer too but this had been his last year in the college and when he had finished he vanished. No one knows where he went and no one has heard from him since. He and Mattie and Luca were going to share an apartment and instead it is only Mattie and Luca living here.

Luca does not have a reason to have stayed. He could have gone home to the neat little house with a yard around it, his family would have been happy to see him and he should miss them, he should want to see them but it was not enough, he did not want to leave. He did not want to go back to where life was small enough for all of it to fit into a neat little house and nothing else but the sky overhead. There is too much that he has done here and too much that has happened and he does not want to have to explain, he would rather stay here in the thick of it, where this is simply the way that life works. He found a job as a cashier in a grocery store and that did not work out and now he is a waiter at a café nearby. On the days he works he wakes up early and he arrives at the café before it opens, he has tea and something to eat—croissants and cheese from the shop next door, or some fruit, or the cook will make him an omelette from whatever bits are left over from the evening before—and then the café opens. He works and at the end of the day he comes back here. Today he does not work. He slept late and when he woke up there was no rush to get out of bed, now there is this cup of tea and after it the day will unfold slowly. He may leave the apartment or he may not; if he does leave he will likely wait for evening, when it is cooler, unless he decides to go for a swim or to lie in the sun in a park. He would go to a park not far from here, it is a bit of green reclaimed from the endless tangle of the city, and there would be trees and children running around and their parents somewhere nearby, to watch over them. Luca would find an open patch of grass and he would have brought a blanket with him, to lie on, and his sketchbook, and that would be the afternoon. He fishes the tea bag out of his mug with his fingers and he puts it on the windowsill behind him and he settles more deeply into his chair. It is a flimsy and rickety thing, the chair, once it must have been a nice chair and now it will do for the summer, if he is careful, and whatever happens to it after that does not matter. The college will have opened again and he will have left all of this behind.

When he and Mattie first arrived here the landlady met them on the street outside and let them in. She opened the door and led them up the stairs and there were the beds in the bedrooms, a table and chairs in the kitchen, and pots and pans and whatnot in the cupboards; she showed them where everything was kept and where the light switches were, how the locks on the doors worked. She was a small and tired-looking woman with a long skirt and her hair halfway gone to grey, and Luca and Mattie had some of their things with them in backpacks and more in the suitcases dragging along behind them. They carried one apiece and they passed another back and forth between them as they walked here from the college, and all the rest of their things are stored away somewhere in the cellars of the college. The landlady gave them the keys and she left, and they stood in the kitchen, they decided who would have which bedroom and then they went to unpack, and in the morning Mattie went off to work and Luca went to look for work. His hair is long enough now to tie back, at least most of it is, and he has bought a pack of hair ties to tie it back with. There are bits of it around his ears that are still too short and they drift away from his head but most of it stays, and when he goes into work he knots it up on top of his head and now it is mussed from having been slept on and it hangs loose and listlessly. Amalia is spending the summer with her family. The night before she left they were in his room, and part of the way through the night, when she thought he was asleep, she slipped out of the bed. She dressed, and she went back to her own room, and in the morning a grey car came. The doors opened and one after another her mother and her father stepped out. Luca still wonders how they would have said hello, if they are a family that hugs or kisses or something else altogether, and how they would have loaded Amalia's suitcases into the trunk before they drove away, and maybe there was something Luca could have done for it to have happened differently but he did not. He woke up in the morning and he had wanted to kiss her goodbye, and he sat alone in the kitchens with a cup of tea and a bowl of oatmeal he could not bring himself to do anything with and that was that, Amalia was gone.

She is spending the summer with her family. Luca has a telephone number he can call, except that when he does she is usually not there, or busy somewhere else, there are whole weeks where she is busy somewhere else and sometimes Amalia will call him but she feels too far away when she does. They talk when they can and for as long as they can and it never feels like it is long enough. Amalia has to go and they hang up, and Luca gets back to whatever it was he was doing before. He drinks the last of his tea and he puts the mug on the windowsill beside the tea bags that have accumulated there. He will go back inside soon, but not yet. There are birds in the alley, twittering and squabbling among themselves, and there is a tree somehow growing behind one of the buildings facing him. Its leaves rustle as if there were some sort of a breeze. He sits a moment longer, as if he is waiting for something to happen, and when it does not he stands and goes back inside.

Part Three

At last, the summer has come to an end, the year is about to begin and Luca and Mattie are outside, standing on the street in front of their apartment with all of their stuff packed back into their suitcases. They have locked the door behind them and they have left the keys in the mailbox, where the landlady will find them, they have gone for breakfast at the café where Luca had worked so that Luca could say goodbye, and now, at last, they are making their way back to the college. They are almost to the lane, they are on the street that will take them to the gate and then to the college; they are so very nearly there that it is a pang in their chests and then here is the gate—it is not quite closed and swinging on its hinges, of course, and though they have not come that far it is not a good day to be carrying suitcases through the streets, there is too much sun for that and now their foreheads are slick with sweat and their clothes are sticking to their skin and they stop, they take a moment to rest and then Luca pushes the gate open. He holds it while Mattie brings their suitcases through and once Mattie and all their things are through he lets it swing almost shut again behind them and here is the lane, like they remember it. They walk one in front of the other with a bounce in their step, they follow along as the lane winds toward the college and in the courtyard at the end of the lane the tree is in bloom, leaves lightly dust its branches and there are flowers too, nestled in among the leaves, small delicate bunches of them that will be gone soon; summer is ending and soon there will be a coolness in the air, soon they will need sweaters but for now they are wearing t-shirts and little else, and they go into the college and into the reception hall, where the secretary is sitting at his desk to welcome the new students trickling in one by one from the lane.

He is sitting here, at this end of the room, and across from him are the new students who have just come through the door; there are chairs set out for them to sit in while they wait to see him but there are more of them than there are chairs and so some of them are standing, and they all look bewildered and lost, and even if they are too nervous to remember it they are all of them hopeful. Luca remembers when he was here, last year, he was standing by the door because he was too nervous to sit and now he is standing again, but this time it is because there is nowhere left to sit, and he watches as the secretary calls the new students one by one to his desk. They sit across from him and they look so small sitting across from him, like they are no longer sure how to be all of themselves, and the secretary asks them for their names and then he goes looking for them on one of the lists on his desk, and when he has found them he turns to a cupboard on the wall. Inside there are rows of keys hanging on hooks and his fingers move along one row of keys and then another, he lightly taps every key as his fingers go past, as if he ever so briefly considers every one of them before he chooses which one to pluck from its hook and slide across the surface of the desk toward the student sitting across from him, and then he explains how to find the door it opens. Go through this door here and down that corridor until you come to the great hall, don't worry, you will know when you've found it, and there will be a door on the wall across from you and a little to the left, and it is not that door, it is the door next to it, you go through that door and you will be in a corridor that will take you to the north wing, follow it for three turns, left and then right and then left again— he stops sometimes, and starts over if he needs to and whoever it is across from him nods along and somehow understands, or at least pretends to, and when the secretary finishes he gestures with an open hand to the door beyond him and off they go, one after another, into the college and into the year.

The secretary is young, he does not look that much older than the students who come and sit across from him and if it were not for his suit and his neatly cut hair he could almost be mistaken for one. He wears thin-framed glasses and behind them his eyes are grey and there is a liveliness to them, and if it were not for his suit and his serious glasses there would be something impish about him. A smile flickers quickly across his face and he says, hello Luca, hello Mattie—there is no need to ask for their names, he remembers them, it is part of what he does, he remembers names and faces— and then he looks down to look through a list, he finds their names and he turns to the cupboard of keys. He chooses one and then another and here are your keys, and here is where to go, he spells out their routes through the college and they nod along as he goes, and they will walk together to the great hall and there they will say goodbye. Mattie will go toward the workshops, where there are the tools for fashioning nearly anything she could think of, and her room will be there too, above them, it is a room that was a place to keep the kinds of things the caretakers keep around but they have cleared it all out to make a room for her; they cleaned the window and swept the floor, then put in a bed and a dresser and a drape to draw over the window at night, and there is a rickety set of steps leading down from it to the workshops so that she can come down to work on whatever she ends up working on whenever she likes. Luca goes up the stairs and past the grand old doors leading into the gallery—it is empty now, inside there are only the walls waiting for whatever happens this year—he goes around the great hall and through a smaller and simpler door, and through it is a narrow corridor with walls painted white and bare bulbs hanging from the ceiling every few steps, and under his feet the floor is uneven and creaks like he remembers and this is home. He has come home. The corridor leads him along, it twists and turns through the college, it takes him to a staircase and he goes up and then a bit to his left, and he has come to a part of the college where there are studios for students to work in. He is at one end of a corridor and it goes along and it turns and it turns again and then again, it circles above a courtyard, Luca can look down and see a door that leads out into it—he can see the door from up here but no one is quite sure how to find it from the inside, and since that door is the only way into the courtyard no one has been in it for ages and all there is down there are birds and dead leaves. Luca walks along the corridor and all along it are doors leading into studios, if they are on one side they look down on the courtyard and if they are on the other they look out onto the roof of the college and then the roofs of the buildings around the college, and then after those roofs all the roofs of all the other buildings in the city stretching off into the distance. Luca counts the doors as he goes and after he has turned once and gone past two doors he stops at the third, he opens this door and here is a studio, and inside is the trunk with all the things he left here and then everything else besides, all of the stuff that has accumulated here over the years that is in heaps all along the walls, like there is in every studio here; there are windows all along one of the walls, and a bed, and the walls have been painted white so many times it is hard to tell what they are made of under all the layers of paint, and hanging from the ceiling is an ornate chandelier. Luca stands under it and he wonders what this room could have been before, to have had a chandelier in it, or if the caretakers took the chandelier from some other part of the building to put it here, and if they did he wonders why they would have done that, if it really had been them who did it. It makes him wonder what he will make of this place, because it is his, for now, and it is exciting to have a place to do anything he likes with.

He drops his backpack and his suitcase and now it is the middle of the afternoon, and tomorrow he will meet with his professor and they will talk about what Luca will be doing this year but mostly they will just say hello, because it has been a long time, and later today there will be supper—the cooks were already starting to prepare it when he arrived, because they like to make something especially extravagant for the first day back. Luca heard them bustling about and he could not tell what it was they were making but he could smell it, and it will still be a while before it is ready, and between now and then is the entire rest of the afternoon and he wonders if Amalia is here yet. The last time they talked on the phone she said she would be here today and she may have already arrived, or if not she will be arriving soon; all the time Luca had been walking through the college he was hoping Amalia would see him and call out, and he would have stopped and they would have stood facing one another again and just thinking about it happening makes his knees wobble. Even the feel of her name in his mouth is enough to take all the weight out of him and leave him feeling silly and afraid.

He wonders where they will find one another, he wonders if he will sleep here tonight, in his room, and if he will sleep alone, and he hopes he will not but what if they do not find one another in time. Amalia will not have the same room she had last year either, so Luca does not know where he would look if he were to go out looking for her but he wants to anyway, just to be looking for her, just to be doing something with the feeling in him but he should unpack, he should make the bed, because what if they found one another and they came back here and the bed was unmade, that would not be any good, so he makes the bed but he does not unpack, because that can wait. He puts his suitcase and his backpack on top of the chest of drawers and that will do for now, and it will end up doing for a while—he has been living out of a backpack and a suitcase all summer and he has gotten used to it—and he leaves, he goes out into the college and he is not sure where he is going to go and that feels right. He has no idea where he should go, where he should look, and so why not wander; he drifts here and there through the endless corridors, sticking his head in through any door that catches his eye, taking in whatever is there to be seen and when he has had his fill of it, when he is satisfied he remembers this place and it remembers him and everything is still where it should be, he wonders what Mattie is up to, so he wanders toward the workshops, in case she is there, and she is not and she is not up in her room either, or at least there is no answer when Luca calls up the stairs, so Luca goes down toward the great hall. He passes other students in the corridors, some of them are new and others are coming back after the summer, and he recognizes some of them, and they recognize him, and they say hello when they do and sometimes they stop and ask one another what was your summer like, and what about yours, and sometimes he sees a new student whispering the secretary's directions aloud, so as to not forget them, or just wandering lost through the college somewhere between worried and somehow still hopeful. He comes to the great hall and the light coming down through the skylight falls warmly on his skin and it is quiet but not quite, there is a rustling all around him, there are the students trickling in from the reception hall and others who have come back down from their rooms, Luca watches them moving through the hall around him, and there is the sound of them in all the spaces just on the other side of the walls too, and he missed those sounds—he did not realize it until now, he did not even remember having noticed it until now but the soft patter of footsteps moving through this place is so unlike how the city outside sounds and he missed it dearly.

It is nearly time for supper, Luca can feel it in his belly; it is not quite ready but it will be soon enough so Luca goes down to the kitchens and there is tea set out for anyone who happens to come by between meals and so he sits with a cup of tea. It is a bit too hot and he blows on it before sipping it and slowly the kitchens fill up around him, a roast comes out of an oven and onto a platter, one of the cooks brings it to a counter and another is ready with carving knives in hand and the caretakers are here, wearing their coveralls and sitting at a table in a corner, wrapping up a game of cards after their own suppers. The one with a moustache is stroking his moustache and the other one's eyebrows are bunched up thoughtfully, there are some students already here and all the rest are still arriving, some are familiar and others are new and even though Luca looks up every time someone comes through the door somehow none of them are Amalia. Luca is really not very good at being patient, the feeling inside him is too much and he is starting to ache from it, and at least supper is ready—the meat is thinly sliced and arranged on platters and there are potatoes and a salad and tranches of freshly baked bread to mop up the gravy. Luca gets up and he gets in line, he gets a plate and a fork and a knife and one of the cooks places a slice of the roast on his plate and another a baked potato dressed with sour cream and chives and dusted with ground pepper, he pours himself another cup of tea, he goes back to where he was sitting before and as he sits down he sees Mattie on the other side of the kitchens. Her glasses have slipped down her nose and she is looking around, as if she is looking for someone, and when she sees Luca she says, there he is, he's over there, and she points and Amalia is with her.

Mattie and Amalia must have been behind him in the line to be served, they have their trays in their hands and they had been looking for a place to sit when Mattie saw him, and they come over to where Luca is sitting, it takes them forever and as they are coming close Luca wonders if he should stand or if he should stay sitting and it is too late, he is already standing and reaching out and Amalia comes to him, somehow she has the good sense to put her tray down on the table first and she comes to him, she buries her face in the crook of his neck and she holds him, she strokes his back and she holds him, and when they sit down they sit close beside one another and they almost eat—it is supper, after all, and they should eat except they cannot quite stop smiling and when at last supper is over they say good night to Mattie and then they slip away. They go up from the kitchens and through the great hall and they almost make it back to Amalia's room without stopping to kiss—Amalia stops, they are in the middle of a flight of stairs and she takes Luca's face in her hands, she draws him to her and she kisses him, and their mouths are wide and their breath comes ragged and then they are in Amalia's room, and they get tangled up in their clothes, because sometimes it takes altogether too long to undress and right now neither of them has the patience for it and so they make a mess of it, and later, when they are lying breathless and naked and sprawled out in her bed, Amalia inspects Luca's hair and how long it has grown, and Luca lies between Amalia's legs, his head resting on her breast and his hand roaming the soft flesh of her belly.

They lie adrift in one another and eventually they fall asleep, neither is sure exactly when, and in the morning Luca wakes up, he slips from the bed and Amalia rolls over into the space he left behind him; he stands up, groggily, and once he is standing he looks around for where his clothes have wound up. They are in a knot on the floor and he has to kneel to untangle them, and he dresses, he pulls on his underwear and then his jeans and the hair tie he used yesterday is still knotted up in his hair; he works it out and he ties his hair up again and Amalia has woken up, she has rolled over and propped her head up in her hands to watch as Luca dresses. He is clumsy and a little awkward when he moves, except when he forgets to be, like when he is focused on something and he is not paying attention to what he is doing, only that there is something to be done, then he moves easily, and as he pulls his t-shirt over his head Amalia takes in the curve of his belly going down into his jeans and his shoulders working to fit into a shirt that is really too small, and when she rolled over she slipped some of the way out from under her blanket, and here is the arch of her back and the rise of her hips and the light on her skin and her eyes are as inscrutable as they ever were. She watches with her slight smile playing across her lips and it is as if she never left, as if she had not been away for the entire summer, except that she was, and that is still between them like a kind of a bruise neither wants to touch. Luca dresses and when he is dressed he bends over the bed, to kiss Amalia goodbye, and Amalia rolls over onto her back so she can reach up with both of her hands to touch him, and Luca comes close to sinking back down with her but he does not, somehow he finds his way to the door and out through it.

He comes out the door and he cannot keep himself from smiling, he goes down a flight of stairs with a lightness in his step and at the bottom of the stairs is a door and then here is the college, here is everything he left behind at the end of last year and here he is, back again, and Amalia is back and everything is right again. He can still smell her on his skin, and the smell is both new and so familiar, and he drifts contentedly through the college—he does not have time to go down to the kitchens for breakfast, and he may regret that later but for now he is glad for the extra little bit of time he got to spend in bed, and he makes his way somewhere else; he slips through an unremarkable door and he closes it behind him, carefully, so the only noise it makes is the latch falling back into place, and here is where the professors have their offices, here is the place where they come when they are not to be found anywhere else. Even though it is the morning and outside the sun is bright the light here is dim, the walls and the dark wood of the floor soak it up and leave the place sombre and contemplative and Luca steps lightly here, because it would be wrong to be anything but quiet here, and all the doors are tucked into the folds of the walls, like they have been discretely hidden away; Luca passes one door and then another and on the doors there are small plaques, like might accompany the exhibits at a museum, and every plaque has the name of a professor engraved upon it. From the other sides of the doors Luca sometimes hears quiet things being done, like pages turning or pens scratching paper, and here, behind this door, someone coughs, dryly, and then Luca hears a sound that could be a handkerchief snuffling about a nose and he goes a little further and then he stops in front of another door and he knocks, and he fidgets while he waits for it to open and when it does here is his professor.

She has a shawl draped over her shoulders and she says, good morning, and then, come in; she turns away and Luca comes in, she quietly closes the door behind him and it is cluttered inside with books and loose papers and drawings lying here and there, where there is space for them—there are some spread out on a desk, along with piles of books, and the desk is broad and made of oak and there is a simple chair behind it, there are curtains over the windows to soften the light coming into the room, and off in the other corner is a sofa with a low table in front of it and an armchair beside it. This room is not a small room, it could not be and still hold everything inside it but it feels small, or it feels like it must be small, because of how close everything inside it feels, it is a feeling a little like how the professor speaks, quietly and gently. The drawings are mostly the professor's own, and Luca can see something of this old woman in them, something like how she would hold a pencil, delicately, with only the tips of her fingers, to carefully and precisely make a certain sort of line, and it shakes sometimes, because sometimes she cannot keep her hands from shaking, but still there is something careful and precise about it. In all her drawings there is something else, something that Luca can feel in them but does not quite understand—he cannot see how her eyes drift away from whatever it is she is looking at when she draws, how a memory rises up to take its place. It is not something he can imagine, not now and not for years to come; he is much too young to know how long a life can be, and how much it can contain, and so for now he has only the vaguest sense of what it is he is looking at, and behind him the professor settles in the armchair and she waits for Luca to finish looking around and sit beside her on the sofa, and when he sits there is a teapot with steam rising from it on the table between them; it is sitting on a platter with two cups and a pot for sugar and a small pitcher of milk and a small plate with biscuits beside it. The professor leans forward to pick up the teapot and pour, she is careful to keep the ends of her shawl and the sleeves of her cardigan tucked away while she does, and after she has poured them tea and they are sitting with their cups in their hands she asks Luca what he would like to do this year. There will be classes to go to but not many, because there is so much more to learn than what can be learned in a classroom, so what else, what else would you like to do, and Luca sits back, he sips his tea and of all the things he has learned, of all the things he has wanted to do in the time he has been here—there have been no end of things, how to make a sculpture shape the space around it, how to select paper for drawing based on its texture and what it will be like to draw on it, and how that will change what the drawing becomes, how to paint as if it was the movement of the brush that mattered, not the marks that it left—of all these things, what he keeps finding himself coming back to, without ever meaning to, is the sky.

Not the sky that is here but the sky that he remembers, that he has not seen in over a year and that he has still not forgotten, not even a little, and why is that. That is what the professor would say, if he were to try to say something about the sky, about how he would like to lie on his back on the roof of the school with the sun shining lazily down and draw it, so he ducks his head to sip at his tea and he tries to think about why, and the professor sits and she watches him with her distant eyes, patiently, and he tries to remember that other sky, and not just the sky but what it was like, to live in a tidy little house under it, and how it felt like the whole of his life and everything else fit under it and that was it. How he could see everything under that sky, he did not even have to try, it was just how it was there, it was not all tangled up and buried inside of itself like it is here, it was a small, simple place that went on forever. And he remembers once, when he was looking out the windows of one of the studios and he saw the windows in the building across from him; he remembers wondering then what was there, behind them, what sort of lives unfolded there and what would it be like, what would he be able to see from out there, and how he felt in that moment a yearning. How he did not want to just stay within the walls of the school, he wanted to reach as far as he remembers the sky reaching, he wants to see this place come together like his home did, under its sky, and he says what he would like to do—his voice rises as he says it, to try to fill out the idea, to give it the substance it needs and he does not know if he does, if what he is saying makes any sense, and the old woman facing him listens as he says that he wants to draw the college, all of it, she sips at her tea and she nods when it is right to nod, and she listens, kindly, to what this boy has to say and when he has finished, when his half-formed idea hangs between them and they both have a sense of what it might be like to follow it, to see where it might go and what it might become, Luca sits with his eyes wide and uncertain, almost trembling, because he does not know if he has said enough, it is all that he has to say and what if it is not enough, he sits and he hopes and he waits for the professor to say something. It is a moment where anything might happen and the old woman sips at her tea and, in her quiet voice, she says, yes.

And then it is another day, and Luca sets out from the college, he goes out the door leading to the lane and then at the end of the lane here is the gate, he slips through it and almost shuts it behind him; he stands still for a moment, to look around, at how the street moves and how there are still points that do not, at how the street eddies around them, the street lights and the traffic lights, the benches beside bus stops and here is someone standing at a corner playing a wheezing old accordion; Luca stands still and he tries to take it all in, he tries to understand and still he does not, but at least over the summer he has figured out how to try. He looks around him and then he turns to the left, he walks down this street and then down another, and this one is quieter, more still, it is lined with the façades of houses and occasionally there is a tree, or someone who is out for a walk, and Luca walks until he finds a way to slip behind this street; here is a gap between two houses and no fence to keep him from going through it, and on the other side of this street is the college, or rather here is a lane buried in the middle of a city block and on the other side of the lane is a wall, an old wall rising up higher than the houses on the street where Luca just was. The wall is one of the walls of the college, it is made of crumbling brick and dotted with windows that look in on what happens inside it. He slips his backpack off his shoulders and he sits, he takes a sketchbook out—it is a new sketchbook, this is the start of something new and so he has a new sketchbook to go along with it, and he has come here to sit behind these houses so he can look at this stretch of wall and look up at these windows, so he can draw them, and what he really wants to draw is so much more than this but he is starting here, because he has to start somewhere; he will draw the windows first, he will get a feel for them and how their frames sit in the wall, and then he will draw the walls, the weight of them and their purpose, what it was and what it is now, and what that makes of them, because purpose leaves marks, they are not always easy to find but they are there and they are important for what he wants to do.

To start he wants to draw the college, all of it, or if not literally all of it then what it would be like if it were somehow possible to see all of it at once, and see how all the various bits of it fit together, and he is starting here, with this wall and these windows, and slowly he will make his way around it; anywhere he can find a place where he can see a part of it he will sit down with his sketchbook and eventually he will go all the way around it and he will have put the whole sprawling mess of it to paper, and then when he has done that he will see if he can recognize in it anything about what it is like to be inside the college, he will see if he can take everything about the college, all the tangled, rambling mess of it, and stitch it into something that feels whole. But not yet, now he is still feeling out these particular windows, and the backs of the houses facing them—there are yards behind them, he thinks they are a bit too small to be properly called yards but there are fences around them and so they are yards, and there are knots of weeds and brambles creeping their way up the fences, and the backs of the houses still look asleep or if not asleep then empty, because the people who live in these houses have all gotten up to go to work or wherever it is they go for the day and their houses have sunk into silence without them. Luca sits down with his back to a fence and he looks up at the wall of the college and he draws, and when he has finished, or at least when he has drawn all he is going to draw today, he has drawn the wall and the windows looking out from it and he has also drawn the fence he was sitting against and the green growing over it and what he could see of the yard on the other side of it. He had not planned to do that but he did, and he closes his sketchbook, he puts it back into his backpack and he leaves; he stands up and he swings his backpack onto his back and he finds his way back to the street, he walks to the end of this street and turns onto another street and on this street he comes across a bakery. He did not have time before he left the college to have breakfast—there should have been time but there was a kiss instead, and then what that led to, and Amalia promised to save him something but he is hungry now, because a cup of coffee is not a breakfast and that is all that he has had. He stops, he steps into the bakery and he was going to ask for a single croissant, which would be enough to get him back to the college, and instead he buys a half-dozen and a pot of jam so he and Amalia will have something to share. The baker has thick arms and strong hands, she is wearing a plain dress and an apron that strains to hold all of her in and after Luca has paid and she has pushed the cash register drawer shut she reaches into a tin beside it and she gives Luca a treat in a cellophane wrapper, because he seems like a good boy, and Luca blushes and says thank you and they wish one another a good day and Luca goes the rest of the way back to the college with a sweet melting on his tongue.

He comes to the gate and then to the end of the lane, he comes back into the college and here is the secretary sitting at his desk, drawing up a schedule for next week's studio allotments, and Luca carries on past him, toward the library, and he does not notice at all how the corridors wind and turn, or when they fork or cross one another between here and there; he does not have to pause to think about which way he has to go, he chooses without seeming to and he says hello whenever he passes someone he knows, and once when he says hello to someone he stops to say something else too and then he remembers where he is going and why he was hurrying, he says goodbye and he hurries on and then he has come to the library. He says hello to the librarian and here are the rows of shelves and somewhere in among them is a creaking flight of stairs that leads down and this is where Amalia is, this is where she goes first thing in the morning. She comes down the stairs and she turns on the lights, and they stutter and stumble between on and off before finally settling on being on and even with the lights on it is still gloomy down here, the lights only almost pick the shelves out of the surrounding dark. The shelves are not like the shelves in the library above, with their books neatly arranged and exactly where they ought to be, these are the archives, and where anything is down here depends on where there was room when it was brought down, and somewhere down here is the last book Amalia needs. She has been all through the library and she has found every other book she needs, except for this one, and she could not find it in the library above because, it turns out, it was not there to be found. It was moved to the archives and now it is packed away in a box that might have been labelled, or not, before being brought somewhere down here and placed on any one of these shelves, and chances are that she does not really need this book, that all the other books she already has will be more than enough and yet she comes down here every day. She has a hunch about this book, that there will be something in it that will help to stitch together all the other parts of the essay she is to write this year— she is in her last year and so she has a final project to do, and for her it is to write an essay on a topic of her choosing but first she has to research it, and then to write it, and then to present it before all the professors and they will have their say as to whether it is good enough to pass and she is sure that this book is the key to the whole thing. So she comes down the stairs in the morning and she turns on the lights and there is a desk at the bottom of the stairs, before the shelves and the gloom start. The desk has a lamp on it and when she first came down there was a thin film of dust on the surface of it but not anymore, she spent a good deal of her first week down here tidying up—she comes down the stairs and she sits at the desk, she has a box open in front of her and she looks through it. She takes out one thing after another and piles everything neatly beside the box and mostly they are folders and sometimes they are not, there are all manner of things that are sent to the archives and only some of them fit into folders. Luca comes down the stairs and he rests his hands on Amalia's shoulders, he says hello and Amalia lifts her head and Luca bends to kiss her on the cheek, he asks her how her morning has been and the book she is looking for is not in this box either, everything is going to have to go back into it and then she will have to try another, and she tries to say it with a shrug and a smile but there is something frustrating about how long it is taking, how much time she has to spend down here in the almost dark and the musty, earthy cold that seeps in through the walls. And she has something for Luca to eat, like she promised, and Luca has the croissants and jam from the bakery and they could leave, just for a little while, they could go somewhere else to eat even though Amalia says she should not, but she has been down here for hours and maybe a break would do her good, it is starting to feel like she has been down here forever but first, before they go, she has to make sure everything she has taken out of the box is somewhere she will be able to find it when she comes back and after she has done all that they go.

They go back up the stairs and Amalia tells the librarian she will be right back, she just needs a bit of fresh air, and the librarian shoos them along and they go up a flight of stairs that once went somewhere and does not anymore, there is the landing at the top, and maybe there had once been a door here or maybe the stairs had carried on even higher and now there is only a landing here and nothing else. They sit cross-legged with their knees touching and the food they have brought laid out in their laps—Amalia has two boiled eggs left over from breakfast, and a cook saw her wrapping them in a napkin to take away with her and gave her an orange to go with them, and Luca has the croissants he bought and they eat; they shell the eggs and they peel the orange with their hands, they dip bits of the croissants into the pot of jam and Amalia tells Luca what she has found so far today, even though she should probably not be spending all this time trying to find this book, she should be reading the books that she has already found, and taking notes, and starting to put together a draft of her essay and instead she tells Luca about all of the odd little things that someone thought it was important enough to keep, the boxes of letters and the books full of receipts, the notes jotted on a napkin and the invitations to events that have otherwise been long forgotten, and Luca tells Amalia about his morning, and what it was like to sit in the city and just draw, or at least he tries to, because he is not sure himself what it was like but even though he is still in the middle of figuring it out he tries to say something, because he wants to have something to say to her, and she listens; they talk back and forth and they listen and they eat, and everything slowly starts to be a little easier or make a little more sense, now that they have said it out loud to someone who has listened, and when they have eaten all they are going to eat they lick their fingers and put what is left into the paper bag from the bakery—some of the croissants, because Luca got too many, and most of the jam—Luca puts the paper bag in his backpack and they stand up, they dust the crumbs from their laps and they kiss, not in a lingering way, only lightly, almost as if this were the best way to get the crumbs out from the corners of their mouths. Amalia goes back to the library, she smiles and she waves to the librarian on her way back down into the archives, and Luca goes up to his studio.

He comes in and he comes to the middle of the room and he sits on the floor, because he has not yet found a chair, he opens his backpack and he reaches around the paper bag from the bakery— he will take it out later and leave it beside the bed, and it will sit there for a while, unless he gets hungry again and wants something to eat later today but for now he reaches past the paper bag so he can get to his sketchbook, he takes it out and he rolls over so he is lying on his stomach on the floor and propped up on his elbows; he opens the sketchbook and he looks through the drawings, he flips from one to another, and it is not enough, like this they are only drawings in a sketchbook and that is not enough, so after he has looked at them all he tears them out and spreads them out on the floor around him so he can see them all at once, and he lies with them around him, like everything was when he was out drawing, and this is more like what he was trying to explain to his professor. He remembers what it was like to be still, to be able to breathe, to look around, to see the city as something he could just sit back and look at, and to find the college in that stillness, or at least a very small part of it. But more than that there is this stillness, there is the possibility of stopping, and just looking around, of seeing what this place is instead of always being blindly caught up in it, and what if that is what he wants to find, a still place he can look out from. He also wants to put the drawings up on the wall, to see them better, and also because his neck is getting sore from how he has been lying, and if he is going to put them up on the wall then he will need to find pins to put them up with, and while he is out looking for things he should look for a table of some kind too, so that there is somewhere to sit and a proper place to work, and also a chair to sit on while he is working, he must not forget about that. The next time he sees the caretakers he says hello and they nod, because that is what they do; it is in the kitchens, they have just eaten their lunch and Luca is coming down for his, he comes up to them and says, excuse me, and tells them about what he is looking for and he asks where he should look and they mumble to one another, the one with a moustache strokes his moustache and they nod, more to one another than to him, and they say he should ask the secretary about the pins, because he is the one who knows about stationery, not them, but the table, they may know of a table. They will see if they can do something and they leave before all the other students come tumbling down the stairs and then it is later, long after Luca has eaten lunch and then gone to a class, it is the evening and Amalia goes down to the archives again, no matter that it is late, because she still has not found the book and it maddens her that it is taking this long to find it—she is falling behind where she ought to be, she has had meetings with professors and she has not done things that she should have already done by now, and she is convinced it will all work out, that once she finds this book everything else will fall into place, it is just that she cannot find it and she does not know what to do except keep trying, no matter how futile it seems.

Luca is with her even though he does not like being down here, it is too dark and too dank, there is too little light and not enough to see. He sits at the desk at the bottom of the stairs and he watches Amalia pace the shelves, he watches her look in boxes she has already looked in and he sits at the desk with his legs tucked up under him, he has his sketchbook with him and he is drawing idly—

sometimes an idea will come to him and he tries to put it down on the page and sometimes a line intrigues him, and he tries to tease out the shape it hints at but it does not often come to anything, and sometimes when Amalia is working Luca will sit a little way away from her and draw her but not now. She is frustrated and when she is frustrated she falls apart; she is always poised, even when she is naked, even when she is asleep it is somehow still like she is making the effort to carry herself properly and she is not poised now, she is too tired, and angry because she is tired, because she does not want to be tired, she wants to find this book and that is more important than worrying about being tired. The way she moves pulls too hard on her body and she does not care, she paces the length of the shelves and sitting here watching her is almost like watching her break herself apart and Luca does not want to draw her like this, he does not want to see her like this, and besides it is too dark here to be drawing anyway, it is too musty and too cramped and Amalia is too preoccupied for there to be anything else to do and Luca is too tired to be sitting here hunched up on a hard wooden chair. He stands up and he takes a step away, toward the stairs, and then another, he says goodbye but Amalia is distracted—she has to find this book, she has to. Even if she does not really have to, even if she could work around it, and she knows she probably could, she does not want to. She has put too much into finding it to give up on it now and she only almost turns toward Luca to say goodbye, and it pains her to be like this, she does not want to and it makes her more frustrated and her eyes quiver like she is about to cry but she will not, she will not let herself, not with this book still nowhere to be found. She swallows it down and Luca does not know what to do, if he should stay or not, he says goodbye and he climbs the stairs back up to the library.

He wanders aimlessly through the college until he comes to the great hall, and when he comes to the great hall he stops; he is on the balcony looking out over the empty space of the hall and he leans his elbows on the banister and he looks up, up through the skylight and to the sky. It is night and so it is dark, and the lights are lowered in the college at night, because that is how lights should be at night; they are only enough to almost see by and the lights from the city are a glow framing the glass, and the stars are dim and he still wishes he could see them properly, like he could before he came here; he wonders when he will see those other stars again and he knows it will not be soon, and so he looks up at this sky instead and he misses the other stars and the vastness of their sky, how everything was clear and simple and everything had its place under the wide open expanse of it, it is just something he remembers now, and he is not even sure anymore he is remembering it properly, and he is trying to make do without and maybe he is close to making it work but right now it does not feel like it and so, out of habit, he looks up to these stars for what comfort they can offer. The college is quiet around him, anyone who is still up and doing things is doing them quietly, carefully, from a kind of respect for the night and how a night should be. Below Luca people pass through the great hall and it is like none of them are really people, they are all like ghosts, or shapes sliding through the dim, and Luca is just one of them, he could be anyone standing here and looking up at the sky and it is a relief. It is a relief to have stepped away from every little thing that is happening, and to just look up at the stars and not have to be anything else, and when he has had his fill of it and he is ready to leave, when he is ready to step back into life, he turns away. He makes his way slowly up to his studio, he opens the door and he closes it behind him, he threads his way through all the stuff on the floor between him and the bed and with a sigh he flops down on it. He does not undress and he does not close his eyes, he is still a little unsettled but he is more tired than unsettled now, and he lies on his back with his hands resting on his stomach and his feet hanging over the edge of the bed, he looks up at the ceiling in the dark that is not actually all that dark and eventually he falls asleep.

—

In the morning he wakes up to the sound of the caretakers coming in through the door. He does not know it is the caretakers, he hears the door open and he hears a shuffling and something heavy bumping against the door frame and he sits up, startled and completely awake, and here are the caretakers with a table stuck in the door between them. They brought it up from wherever they had found it and they fit it through any number of doors between here and there, but it is apparently not so straightforward a task to get it through this one last door. They have put it down with half of it in the room and the other half still out in the corridor and now they are working out how to get the rest of it through. One of them is inside and the other is still in the corridor, and while they are puzzling over what to do next Luca picks his jeans up from the floor, because sometime in the night he managed to take them off, he pulls them back on again and he comes to help them. Together the three of them turn the table this way and that, to get the legs and then the length of it through the door, and then the other two legs and then it is done. The table was likely a table in a magnificently elaborate dining room before it found its way up here, and the three of them carry it to the centre of the room and then a little further, so more of it is in the light coming through the windows; they put it down and one of the caretakers wipes his hands together and the other wipes his hands on his overalls, they step back from the table and they look around and they mumble between themselves. One of them points up at the chandelier and they both look up at it and perhaps they want to ask Luca what he thinks of it without being sure of how to go about actually asking and Luca jumps in anyway, he says that he likes it, he likes the light that it makes, how it falls more evenly over the room than if it were just a regular light and the caretakers nod, as if that makes sense, or at least it is something for them to think about and they turn to leave and Luca says thank you, and one of them half turns and he would have tipped his hat, if he had been wearing one—he is not today but some days he does, and that is the sort of thing he does with it when he is wearing it—and they go, and Luca is left alone again except that now he is awake.

There was the fright of waking up and then the work of having helped with the table and now he is too awake to go back to bed, even if he would like to lie still for just a little while longer. The caretakers close the door to the studio after them and he looks over at the bed one last time and he sighs, because even though it is early it is not that early, and down in the kitchens breakfast will be ready. He runs his hands through his hair, so that it is a bit less messy, he ties it up in a knot and he goes down to the kitchens, and there are other students already here, sitting here and there; there are not enough of them to fill the place because it is much too early for most everyone here to be awake. The few students who are here sit in small groups or they sit alone, and there is no line to wait in, Luca gets a tray and a cook serves him a bowl of oatmeal with blueberries and blackberries and brown sugar sprinkled on top, he pours himself a glass of orange juice and a cup of tea, he carries his tray to a table and he eats without saying anything or thinking about much of anything in particular. He moves his oatmeal around in the bowl while he chews and he sips at his tea in between mouthfuls, and when he has finished his oatmeal he drinks all his orange juice in one go and he wonders if Amalia has already eaten or if she has not, because this is about when Amalia usually gets up, and if he should wait for her or not. Amalia will sometimes skip breakfast so she might not show up at all, and she was up late so she might sleep in and Luca is still tired, and there is everything he has to do today and then everything after that and it is like a weight, and instead of anything else he only feels tired and it drags on him, he wants to be swept up in all of this but everything has become too heavy for that, and he takes his tray with his dishes on it back to the cooks and he leaves, and on the stairs he feels a twinge in his heart when a girl in a dress passes him—she does not look like Amalia at all but for a moment Luca thought she did, and he is not sure what the feeling was when he did or what it might have meant, if he was happy to have almost seen Amalia or not, or if he is just too tired and there is no time to dwell on it. He leaves the kitchens, he goes out and into the lane, he has his backpack slung over one shoulder and in the mornings there is sometimes a chill that lingers on into the first part of the day so he is wearing a sweater over his t-shirt and he goes out into the city and already there are people out here, the street is thick with them. They are walking one way or the other and they are on their way to work or to wherever it is that they go in the morning, Luca does not know, he does not even recognize any of them and it has become a strange feeling to not recognize anyone. In the college it is different, even the new students who just started this year are starting to be familiar and he recognizes them when he sees them, even if he does not know their names or who they are, and for these people out here, in the city, he is only a boy wearing a shabby old sweater and it feels odd to him to be this out of place.

He has been all around the college and from all the drawings he has done so far he could start to pull together what it might look like if it were somehow possible to see it, all of it, and all at once, and that would be what he had set out to do but now it is not enough to just do that. He wants more, there is more out there, in the city, and he wants to see it, to sit with it and draw it, and so he keeps going out, he keeps going further and every time he goes further he finds more places to draw. First there were the places he could see from the places he had already drawn from, and that was like a game of hopscotch from one hidden place to the next and slowly, gradually, as he got further and further from the college the secret parts of the city spread out across the walls of his studio. He does not know what to make of all this or how to fit it all together but he trusts that it does, because it does, it is happening all around him and he can see that it does, even if he does not understand how, it is still happening, and he has come out of the gate and he can go one way or the other down the street and it does not matter which, either will take him somewhere new. He steps out into the street and he is swept along with everyone else who is going this way and he does not look where they are all going, he looks around him instead, he looks for places he could sit and draw from—there are the shops along the street, there are the windows of the offices and apartments over the shops, looking down onto the street, and behind them, facing away from the street, there are other windows, or perhaps a balcony, or a fire escape looking out over some place behind the street. Sometimes he sees doors tucked between two shops, they are not marked with anything more than a number for an address and they could be doors that lead to stairs that go up to the apartments above the streets, and he will find his way into some of them; he will learn what a street looks like from just over the heads of the people walking along it, he will sit tucked in the corner of the window of a shop, to see their faces closer up. A little girl will want to stop to look at him, her hair will be in pigtails and she will reach out one hand to touch the window and her parents will tug on the other, and for a moment she and Luca will look one another in the eyes and then she will be swept away.

For now, Luca winds through the streets and eventually he comes to the café he worked at over the summer, he comes in and he says hello to the cook and the waitress is not someone he knows, she started after Luca had left so the cook introduces them, and they say hello and how are you and then Luca finds a seat. The waitress brings him a cup of coffee and he starts to draw the way the city stretches out from the window he is sitting beside and he wonders where he could get to from here; occasionally, he will have a sip of coffee and when it is done and it is time to head back to the college he puts his sketchbook and his pencils back into his backpack, he pays for his coffee and he steps back out into the street. His eyes are bleary and the skin under them is too dark, it almost looks bruised, he is not sleeping enough and he is likely wearing himself out but it does not matter, or he wishes it did not matter. He does not want to stop, not while there is still so much he could do—he may be close to figuring out how this place works, everything is about to fall into place and if only he had it in him to get all the way there and it does not matter if he does not, he will try anyway, no matter how it wears on him, and in the end everything will kind of work out. He steps out into the street and it sweeps him up and carries him back to the gate that does not quite close and it leaves him there, and then there is the lane and then he is back inside, he wanders his way through the reception hall and back into the college. Breakfast has ended and all the other students are coming up from the kitchens, they gather together in the great hall and then they slip away, one by one, off into the tangle of the college and whatever is waiting for them there, and Luca stops in the middle of them, to try to see if Amalia is here. She is probably up by now, no matter how late she stayed up looking for the book she cannot find she would not let herself sleep in this late, and if she is up then she might be here, somewhere, except that he does not see her, no matter how hard he looks, so she is likely already somewhere in the college. She might have gone to a class or perhaps she is already down in the archives, again, and if only Luca could go on looking for her, if only there were the time for that, but he has to look over the drawings he just did, he has to pin them to the wall and keep trying to piece together whatever is slowly taking shape in them. He comes up the stairs and in through the door, he takes his sketchbook out from his backpack and he sits at the newly arrived table, he lays out this morning's drawings in front of him and bringing them all together is like solving a puzzle, except that it is an impossible puzzle— he does not know what it should look like or even what it could look like, it could be anything, really, if it is anything at all, all of which only makes it harder. If there were a way they should all fit together that would make it easier, there would be something for him to work toward, but there is not and that makes it a problem he cannot figure out. If he could find Amalia, if he could talk with her then maybe they could figure it out together but now it is too much, he puts his head on the table and outside the sky is flat and grey and he wants to go back to bed, he wants to be warm and asleep and instead there is a class to go to.

It does not start for a little while yet but it is on the other side of the college and it will take him time to get there, and he will have to go past the library, and when he comes to it he does not go past it he steps inside instead. He goes down into the archives and it is dark, the lights have not been turned on, he cannot see the rows of shelves and Amalia is not sitting at the desk. She is not here. Luca had hoped she would be but she is not, and he does not know where else she might be, and even if he did he cannot run off to find her and that leaves him without much to do but carry on to the class he is on his way to. He touches the back of the chair and it is a chair with wheels on the bottom of it, it turns lifelessly when he touches it and he wanted Amalia to be here, he wanted to say hello, he wanted a kiss and instead he leaves. He climbs back up the stairs and he goes through the library and the librarian has just arrived at her desk with a cup of tea in hand; she says good morning to Luca and Luca says good morning to her, and he goes to his class, he sits and he listens like he should, and when it is over he stands to leave along with everyone else who is standing and leaving. He goes back to his studio and here is everything still waiting for him and still waiting to be done and he cannot, not yet. He goes past everything he has to do and he goes to bed instead; he takes off his shoes and then his sweater, they end up being dropped somewhere on the floor, he lies down and takes off his jeans too and all he wants is to be lying down, to be nestled in the softness of the bed, he pulls the blanket around him and curls up and he does not mean to fall asleep but he does. He sleeps and it is still light out when he wakes up, though only barely; he sits up and he does not know what time it is or how long he has slept and it does not matter how long he slept, he should not have slept at all. He stumbles out of bed and he pulls his jeans back on, and a sweater—it is not the sweater he was wearing before, it is one that is closer, it was on one of the bedposts and he puts this one on instead, and he has to look for his sneakers and he wonders if he will be in time for supper if he leaves for the kitchens now. He comes down the stairs and here are the kitchens and supper is nearly over, there are only a few students left and they are all finishing their meals, the cooks have already started gathering the dishes up, to wash them and put them away, but they have not put everything away quite yet. They ladle out a brimming bowl of stew for Luca and there is some pudding left over and Mattie is here, she has finished eating but she is still here and Luca sits with her, and while Luca eats Mattie tells him what she has been doing. She is making paper—the caretakers have cleared a corner of their workshops for her to work in, she has a workbench against the wall and a window over it and trays filled with pulpy mush laid out on the bench, and overhead are lengths of string strung between the rafters with sheets of what is now paper hanging from them, to dry, and drops and splatters of pulp on the floor beneath them. She is experimenting, she is playing with different ways of making paper to see what difference it makes, to find out what sorts of different things paper can be. She is collecting scraps of cloth and seeing what happens when she mixes in different sorts and different sizes of scraps, what difference it makes in the texture of the paper; she is waiting for a batch to dry and this year she spends most of her time there, in the workshops. Luca does not ever go there, he has no need to, and Mattie never comes to any of the places where Luca spends his time so it has been a while since they have seen one another, and it will be another while until the next time and it is a relief to have this moment, to sit here and eat and talk with a friend. They talk about what they are working on, because that is what they have been spending all of their time doing, and they try to talk about other things too, because it has been so long and there is so much they do not know about one another anymore, so much that neither of them so much as thinks about anymore, because neither of them has the time, and it is nice to have a moment to remember those parts of life. Luca's hair is longer and Mattie's hair is shorter, her glasses have broken again and she has fixed them again, and she does not wear mascara anymore—she stopped sometime over the summer, when she had to get up too early to go to work and it took too much time to put it on, and then she got used to not wearing it and so she doesn't anymore and her hands have changed, they are getting broader, and stronger, she has more calluses and after he has eaten they leave together, they go up the stairs one after the other and they say goodbye in the great hall. Mattie goes back to the workshops and Luca climbs the stairs back to his studio; it is not too late to still get some work done but he doubts that he will, he will likely end up lying in bed again, he is too tired but it is not just because he is tired. Even if he does not sleep it would be a relief to not be working on anything, and he comes to the top of the stairs and into his studio and lies down and then there is a knock on the door. It is Amalia, and look, she has found the book she was looking for.

It was not in any of the boxes where she thought it would be, it was put somewhere else and that was why Luca could not find her earlier—she had gone down a narrow, musty corridor that was more a tunnel than a corridor, really, it led to another basement and another barely-lit room and dust gathered in the corners and shelves, rows and rows of shelves, and more boxes, and there were books in most of the boxes, old books and delicate books, and a few boxes of diaries and notebooks, and in others there were papers and letters and notes on napkins and cards to commemorate occasions that at the time were given in passing and who would have thought they would have ended up where they have ended up. The book Amalia was looking for is only almost a book, it is a notebook, like a schoolchild would use for exercises, and it was in a box with other notebooks like it, all neatly tied together into a bundle. Amalia thought it had been a proper book she was looking for but it is not, it is the idea of a book that was supposed to be written but in the end it wasn't, and there is only this book of notes to show for it, and even though it is not at all what she was expecting to find she found it, she has found it, and it is exhilarating and a relief to have found it and she came up to find Luca, to tell him, except that Luca was not here. Amalia knocked but there was no answer and she looked in and there was no sign of him, so she went away. She went back to her room and she leafed through it, and she fiddled about with some of the other things that she had to do but still she wanted to tell him and now, now they are sitting together on Luca's bed and Amalia has the book with her, and she tells Luca all this, and they come closer and closer together and maybe there is something else Amalia is about to say but they have touched, and now their breath is too heavy for words. Luca lifts his t-shirt up over his head and Amalia's dresses are always tricky, Luca is only halfway through undoing the buttons running down the back of it by the time Amalia has got Luca's jeans undone and pulled down to his knees; together they work Luca's jeans around his feet and then there are the last few buttons on Amalia's dress and it too falls away, and they reach for one another, they tumble together and then into the bed and later, it is much later, the college has gone quiet around them and through the windows the sky is clear, there are only the stars, or at least there are the almost stars of the city sky and the cold night air and they are fast asleep.

They are lying almost on top of one another, because the beds in the college are not built to be big enough for two to sleep in, and they have managed to slip out from under the blankets; it is cold and their skin prickles in the dark and Amalia lifts her head up, she pushes her hair away and she reaches for the blankets, she pulls them over the two of them and draws Luca closer to her. Luca is still deep asleep, his hair is still tangled up in a hair tie and Amalia takes his head, she rests it in the crook of her neck and she holds him, and Luca wraps an arm around her waist and snuggles closer and they sleep, and then later it is a morning, a much later morning, whole months have passed and it has gotten warmer, there is no more need for layers of sweaters or leggings or an extra blanket on the bed and Luca comes out of his studio wearing a t-shirt with the sleeves cut off of it, it is probably not quite warm enough yet to be wearing just this but he wants it to be, and if it turns out to be not that warm yet then he is prepared, he has a sweater in his backpack, along with his things for drawing, and he comes out of his studio, he closes the door behind him and in the reception hall he says good morning to the secretary, and the secretary says good morning to him, he asks him how he is doing and Luca is tired, he slept too late and he has missed breakfast and even though he slept in he is still tired, there does not seem to be anything that will help, but he does not say that, because everyone is always this tired by this time of the year, it is just the way it is, he smiles a wan smile and he says he is fine and then he is off into the city.

Where he is going is not far, and between it and the end of the lane is a bakery and Luca stops there to get a croissant, and then at a café a few doors past it for a cup of coffee, and then he is walking down the street with his coffee in one hand and his croissant in the other. He eats the croissant and he sips at the coffee as he walks, he does not seem to be paying any attention to where he is going but halfway down a particular block he stops, he takes one last sip of his coffee and then tosses the mostly empty cup into a garbage bin and here is the opening to a lane. It is not the lane that leads back to the college, it is another lane, another kind of lane in a different part of the city, he steps into it and there is garbage strewn all along it, it has fallen from the bins that are kept back here, and the smell of it hangs in the air and Luca has to pick his way gingerly through it. He has come here because one of the buildings next to this lane is a high-rise, there are a dozen garbage bins heaped together behind it, that is how much garbage comes out of it, and then beyond the garbage bins is the fire escape, and it should not be possible to climb up onto it but it is broken and instead of the bottom step being too high to reach it is resting only a few feet up from the ground and this is why Luca has come here. He sneaks through the bins as quietly as he can, he is, after all, not supposed to be back here, he puts a foot on the bottom step of the fire escape, to bring it the rest of the way down, it comes down with a thump and then Luca is climbing up it, he goes up one flight of steps and then another, he stops once before he gets to the top because he has lost his breath and he needs to rest, and he goes past so many windows that look in on the apartments of this building—every apartment is an identical concrete cubicle and yet every one is different, because of whoever lives inside and what they have done to make that place home, but none of that is of any interest to Luca, or at least not today, he only looks up and he climbs as fast as he can manage until he has reached the roof. This building is one of the only truly tall buildings in this part of the city, it is taller than almost all of the buildings around it and it makes it so that from where he is on the top of this building he can see everything, he can see the whole entire city spread out around him; he gets to the top of the fire escape and he climbs onto the roof, and all of the sounds that the city makes are gone, they are too far away to hear—Luca had gotten used to them, and he only remembers them now because they are gone, there is a strange sort of silence up here and, occasionally, the sounds the birds still wheeling overhead make.

There is a nest of some kind perched on the other edge of the building and fledglings chirping in it, and the winds are stronger up here, they cut through Luca's t-shirt but he does not notice, he can see forever from up here and that is what matters—from up here he can see every place he has drawn, he can see all the winding streets and how they knot and tangle together, all the buildings and everything else and exactly where they are, he can even see the college, it is a speck in the distance, and from here he should be able to fit everything together; it will not be a matter of him having to piece it together himself, he will see the way it actually is and that will be that, what he has to do will be settled, and so he had started to look around for a building as tall as this one and a way to get to the top of it and now here he is and he can see everything, just like he wanted to, and it does not help. The way that things are laid out next to one another does not have anything to do with what he has drawn, there is nothing of how he was there, how he went from one place to another, how it was him sitting in alleyways and perching on windowsills and how that matters, how him being there gave those places a shape that they would not otherwise have had and how that is what is important. It is not something he can see from up here, it is something else entirely and being up here does not help, he is left with the same problem he had before. But at least he got to climb all the way up here, at least he gets to see all of the sky at once; he stays for a while, to be somewhere where the sky reaches as far as it feels like it should, and he wishes that everything else could be this clear and this simply and easily itself and of course that is not how it works here. It is probably not how it ever works anywhere but still he longs for it, and he draws a little bit but not much, mostly he just basks in the wide open sky until eventually he has to leave.

He goes back down the fire escape and out the lane, he goes back to the street and it is a quiet street, there are only apartment buildings along it and he walks to the end of it and it joins with another street that is not so quiet, he steps in among everyone else walking along this other street and when he comes to the gate to the lane leading back to the college he steps through it, and here are the walls, and the windows opening onto the quiet places all along it and then here is the college, here are the steps leading up to the door and the heavy brass knocker planted solidly in the middle of it, and then the reception hall and the secretary sorting the mail. He is standing in front of the letter boxes for the students and putting a letter here and a letter there, and Luca does not have a letter, or at least not yet, the secretary is still in the middle of a quite substantial pile of letters, but Amalia does; Luca tries to see where the letter is from but he cannot quite tell, other than that it looks very official. If he sees her he will tell her that much, that she has a letter, and he goes down to the kitchens to see if he can find another cup of coffee.

The cooks are in the middle of cleaning up from breakfast and there is no coffee left but one of them stops what he is doing and he puts a pot on, and when it is done he brings Luca a cup and some sugar and a small pot of milk. The tables have all already been wiped down and all the dishes gathered and washed and put away and Luca sits and he drinks his coffee with his sketchbook open in front of him. He flips through the pages without really looking at them, just to have what he drew pass in front of his eyes again, so that it settles in properly, and when he has drunk his coffee he stands and he brings his cup back, and the pot for milk; he has a class to go to and if only he did not have a class to go to but he does and he goes, and then the class is over and it is time for lunch, and there are sandwiches with tomatoes and basil and thick slices of cheese, and salad, and one of the cooks is pressing orange juice and Luca sits with a glass of it and a sandwich and he sits and he eats slowly, nibbling at the sandwich and sipping, every now and then, from his juice, and for a moment he is content, he is meeting with his professor tomorrow and he is thinking of what he will say to her, what they will talk about, and then Amalia finds him. She has the letter that arrived for her this morning; it came from another college, a university, one that it is near a town near a forest that is nowhere near here. There is a river that runs between the college and the town and a path winding along beside the river; she went there with her parents over the summer and she tells him how she stayed in a room over a restaurant, and how she had lunch there with a pair of professors from the university—she talked with them about what she was working on and the work that the university does, and if what she wants to do would be the sort of thing that could be done there and the professors there are different from the professors here, she says, they are sharper, more strict, she had to be at her best in a way she does not have to be here and she was nervous she would not be able to pull it off and thrilled that she did, and afterward she walked with her mother and father from the town to the university and they wandered through the campus. It is in a clearing in the middle of the forest and there are trees all around it, it is practically the size of a town all by itself and when she applied she did not know if she would be accepted or if she could go, or if she was accepted if she would go, and Luca did not even remember that she had applied in the first place and now that this letter has come she is going to go, she is going to study there when the year is done.

When she says it she cannot keep from smiling and she has come to tell Luca, and Luca wants to be happy with her or he wants to be happy for her and instead there is a sinking inside him and an emptiness opening and he says, you are going to go. Luca has another year before he is done here, he will still be here next year and Amalia will not. He will be here without her, because she is going to leave, and it wells up inside him and he does not want it to, he swipes at his eyes with the back of his hand, he does not want it to and he wishes it would not, he wants to be happy for Amalia but he is crying. His mouth trembles and Amalia does not understand, she was happy, and Luca says, you are going to go and, oh. She touches his cheek and Luca pushes her hand away and she says, I'm graduating, you know that, and of course Luca knew and it does not matter, he did not think about it or he thought Amalia would stay, somehow, that she would keep studying here or at least stay in this city; she would have an apartment and Luca would sneak out of the college at night to see her and it always seemed so far off anyway, and he did not think about it because it was so far off and then he forgot, because he was happy, he was so swept up in the thrill of it and everything that he imagined was possible that he lost sight of what was actually happening, he stopped thinking about it and then he forgot, and now he is crying, his nose is running and he does not trust himself to speak and he does not want to be here anymore, he wants to be back up in his room, in his bed, and Amalia sits beside him anyway, and he cries and Amalia puts a hand on his back and he does not want Amalia to see him like this, he does not want to be like this. He stands and he should say something but he does not, he does not even try, he leaves, he stumbles out of the kitchens and he leaves Amalia sitting at the table alone.

He stumbles up through the college and all the way to his room, he comes through the door and he closes it behind him and that is all that he can manage. He does not want to do anything, he wants to believe that nothing more will go wrong so long as he does not do anything, so long as he stays in bed and remains perfectly still there is nothing else that can happen, and it gets later anyway, the light gradually bleeds from the room and he starts to feel ridiculous for having been lying here this long. He picks himself up and it is almost dark, the sun has started to set and it is time for supper but he does not want to eat supper, or he does not want to go down to the kitchens and since that is what he would have to do to eat supper then he is not going to eat supper, instead he takes his jeans off and he crawls into the bed and he does not sleep, he lies there with his eyes open and he wants for nothing at all to happen. He just wants to be still, and to breathe, nothing more, and eventually it is later, it could be the middle of the night and there is a knock at the door. It is Amalia, she is standing in the corridor and she knocks on the door, not loudly, only loudly enough to wake Luca if he were sleeping, and Luca starts and he wakes up. He did not realize he had fallen asleep, he raises his head and he turns to look at the door and in the dark he can vaguely see it, or at least the shape of it and he does not say anything, he knows who is there and he wants her to go away. He wants to lie here and sleep, or lie here and not sleep, if he cannot manage to fall asleep again, and Amalia knocks again and still Luca does not say anything. Amalia says Luca, are you there, and Luca turns away, he faces the wall and he wipes his eyes and he does want to say something but he cannot bring himself to, he wishes he would but even if he did he does not know what he could say. Amalia is going away, he needs her and she is going away and his hands curl into fists and he cries, he chokes on it so she does not hear and on the other side of the door Amalia raises her hand to knock again and Luca pulls the blankets closer around him, he shuts his eyes tight and Amalia lowers her hand, she says Luca, please, and Luca is lying with the blankets pulled tight around him and his legs curled up against his body and Amalia goes away. She walks away down the corridor, or at least Luca thinks she does, he does not hear anything else that could be Amalia no matter how hard he tries. He lies still and there is a sound that might be her steps on the stairs but it could be anything and it does not matter what it is, Amalia has gone, and eventually he falls back asleep.

When he wakes up he sits up, he swings his feet out of the bed and puts them on the floor and he stands, and it is an effort to stand, as if the weight of his body has become a burden, but he has to. It is the morning, there is light coming in through the windows and he has to meet with his professor, and before he does he has to pick out the drawings he wants to show to her; he staggers away from the bed and he sits at the table and he had meant to have already done this, it was what he was going to do yesterday but he has only just started to sort through them, there are some set out here and arranged in a way that made sense yesterday but today he cannot see it and it makes him want to cry again but he does not, he does not have the time to. He stands up from the table and there are still some drawings pinned to the walls and he walks around the room taking some of them down—which ones does not matter, he just wants to feel like he is bringing enough—he mixes them in with the drawings he has already chosen and he is trusting to luck more than anything that they will make sense together but he has to, this is all he can manage to do. He has no time for breakfast, no matter that he is hungry, he leaves his studio and he slips through the college and here is the great hall and here is a door, and it is quiet, here where the professors have their offices, it settles over him and on another day it might have calmed him but not today; he hurried to get here and he is out of breath and the sound of it is ragged in his ears and here is another door, he knocks on it and he waits, it feels like forever and then the door opens and here is his professor. She has her shawl draped around her shoulders and she smiles, gently, she says good morning and she holds the door open for him. He comes in and they sit beside one another, Luca on the sofa and the professor settled into her armchair. The professor reaches for the pot of tea on the table between them, she fills the two cups and she gives one to Luca and she sits back in her chair with the other, and she sips carefully at it, because it is still slightly too hot to drink, and Luca sits with his hands cupped around his. There is a wisp of steam rising from it and a small piece of a tea leaf settling to the bottom and he looks into the cup and he has his drawings with him, they are bundled together into a case and he is supposed to take them out, he is supposed to show them and they are supposed to talk about them, it is supposed to help him along. There are all the things Luca is still not sure about and if he could ask questions, if they could talk together and he only needs a moment to gather himself together, if he just had a moment to gather himself together. If he were to nibble at a biscuit, sip at his tea and then wet his lips with his tongue before speaking and he does not. He picks up his teacup and before he can take a sip he starts to cry.

He does not realize it when it starts, tears have already dropped from the corners of his eyes and started down his cheeks and that is when he feels them, and no, please not now, he only needed a moment more and he would have been ready and then he is crying, he hangs his head and he tries to keep himself from shaking or spilling his tea, he tries to breathe without sniffling and his shoulders tremble anyway, he cannot help it, and it is humiliating, he only needed another moment to pull himself together and this should not be happening, please, and the professor says his name, gently, gently but firmly. There is a solidness to her now that Luca would not have thought this slight old woman capable of, she says his name and Luca looks up and his nose is running and his eyes are red and blurred and his hands are shaking, he is still holding onto his cup of tea, he has not spilled any of it yet but he is about to. The professor has put her cup down and first she takes Luca's cup from him, and she puts it back on the tea tray next to hers, and then she turns to face him. She looks at him with her eyes that have been hollowed by the sadness she has never been without, that has left her emptied out but somehow still strong, no matter that she has never felt strong, and she looks at this trembling boy and she asks, Luca, what is wrong, and Luca says Amalia is leaving, she is leaving him and there, it is said and it cannot be anything but true now. The professor nods and Luca wipes his eyes and the professor rests a hand on his arm, and it is a small, frail thing, her hand, it trembles slightly against Luca's skin but it is solid, more solid than Luca feels and they sit together, quietly, and now sadness is something, it is not only an emptiness it is something else too, something she has recognized, that she knows, and now it is something between them and it is not better, it still makes no sense, it is still twisting inside him but maybe it is more bearable, now that he can see it for what it is. Luca wipes his eyes and the professor gives him a handkerchief to blow his nose and they pick up their cups of tea, and, even though the tea has cooled and it is no longer quite as hot as it should be, they drink.

Luca says he is sorry, and the professor smiles a thin, tired smile, and she nods, which is all that she could possibly say. Luca takes his drawings out and he shows them, and they talk, and it feels good to be able to talk about drawing, to talk about something else, as if there is something else that could still matter. After they have said all they are going to say Luca packs his drawings away again, he is going to leave and just before he does, his hand is already on the door, he says, thank you. He does not look back, he cannot bring himself to, it would be too much if he did and he would be a blubbering mess again, he does not even know if the professor hears him but he says it, and he goes through the door and out past all the other doors with plaques with professors' names on them, and then he is back in the great hall, he is back in the college and the day is still happening and everything is still here, waiting for him to come back.

The End

*I*t is a morning, yet another morning, the year is almost over, nearly everything that was going to happen has happened and all that is left is to let everything play out to the end. Luca is in his studio. He slept alone, like he did the night before and the night before that— he spends his nights alone now, he lies curled up in the rickety bed with a thin blanket over him and the windows open, to let a breeze in, and still it is uncomfortably hot; he cannot find a way to lie in bed that is comfortable so he sleeps too lightly, he is too aware of the roof creaking above him and everything else creaking around him and, further away, the endless grumbling of traffic in the streets below. He cannot close his eyes tightly enough to block it out, every night it seeps through the blankets and he cannot shut it out, he is too alone and he is not sure how it came to this—he does not think he wanted it to, he cannot imagine wanting it to but he does not know, or he does know but he will not ever admit it to himself. Amalia is still here, she is still in the college, somewhere. Sometimes Luca is not sure that she is, they have gotten very good at not seeing one another and then sometimes, by accident, they will come across one another; they will be on their way somewhere neither of them would have ever expected it and they are surprised to find one another. If they are going in opposite directions then they will say hello and not much else, they do not stop, they carry on to wherever they were going, and having seen one another will leave knots in their stomachs for the rest of the day. If they are going the same way then they will walk together, there will be a space between them and they will walk and they will try to say something but mostly they do not, they are too painfully aware of the distance between them, and when they can say goodbye and go their separate ways again it is a bittersweet relief.

Once, in the kitchens, when he was still staying in the kitchens to eat, when there was still some kind of hope that things might not end up this bad, they tried to sit together. Amalia came to sit with Luca, she said hello and she sat down, she asked him how he was, how his work was coming, what sorts of places had he found out there, in the city, and he did not say a thing, she asked him what was wrong and he would not answer and she pushed herself away from the table and she turned toward him, she was shaking and there were all the things she could have said and not one of them would have been worth it. Luca watched her almost say one thing and then choke it back, she would try another and then decide not to, not here, not like this. She looked down on Luca with her eyes hard and flat and there was a sadness there, somewhere, but she was not about to show it and Luca could have said something, he knows, he could have done something and it would have made a difference but he did not. He did not want to. He wanted to hurt her, he wanted to see her hurt too, because somehow it had not occurred to him that she would be hurting too, and she stood over him, trembling, he did not say a thing and neither did she. She turned away and she left, and now Luca wakes up in the morning and he is alone, he rolls out of bed and he pulls on a pair of jeans and he gets to work, because that is what is left to do. He does not go out to draw anymore, either he has more than enough drawings to work with or he does not have the heart to go out anymore, whichever it is does not matter, he does not go anywhere, he stays in his studio surrounded by all the drawings he has done and he does not leave unless he has to. He goes down to the kitchens at odd hours, he gets some of whatever food there is to be had at the time and he leaves again. He does not stop to talk to anyone, he takes his food back to his studio and either he eats there or he eats on the way. It has been ages since he has had a bath and he should probably have a bath but it does not seem worth the effort it would take, to go all the way down to the basement just for that. Mattie comes up to see him, sometimes, because of how long it has been since she last saw him anywhere—she knows what has happened, Amalia told her, they are both the kind of people who like to get up early in the morning and so they sometimes sit together at breakfast, and that is when she told her what happened; now Mattie comes up to see Luca, to see how he is doing, and they sit together and they try to talk about what they are working on, because that is safe, there is nothing upsetting about that. She never stays for long, they talk for a little bit and then a silence settles over them, there is more to say but neither of them knows how to and eventually Mattie pushes her glasses back up her nose and she says goodbye, and that she will see Luca later and Luca nods, and he is left to himself again, with all of his drawings scattered haphazardly about him and no idea what to do with any of them.

He still meets with his professor, he has to, to check in on how his work is coming along, and when he does they sit across from one another, he is on the couch and she is in her armchair, and they do not say much. It feels like there is nothing left to say, no matter that there is, there is still so much that he has not yet figured out about what he is working on, but no matter how much of it there is to talk about they sit across from one another in silence, sipping at their tea, and when their tea is done Luca looks up helplessly, and the professor knows, there is not anything else she can say but at least she knows. After, he goes back up to his studio, to try to work, and it gets darker, and darker, and then it is night; he takes off his jeans and his t-shirt and he curls up in the bed until it is morning again. He wakes up and pulls on a pair of jeans, he sits at the table and the air in his studio is hot and stuffy, no matter that the windows are open, and it still smells like unwashed clothes. His drawings are pinned to the walls and spread out on the table in front of him, there is not much of the year left and he still has not figured out how to piece them all together; they lie jumbled together on the table and that is all, there is no order to them other than where it is they are lying now. He sits in front of them and he looks at them and he has already looked at them, like this and every other way he could think of and it is always the same, they are just jumbled together and he holds his head in his hands and he wonders how he ever could have thought that he could make any sense of this. He remembers how excited he had been, how he would go on and on about it with Amalia and how it made sense then, when it was being whispered about between the two of them, and if he could talk with her then maybe it would make sense again, she would listen and then say something absolutely right and everything would come that much closer to fitting together and he stops himself, because he does not want to be thinking about her, not anymore. He sits at the table and he looks at the drawings in front of him and he wishes there were something more there than what he can see and of course there is not. They are what they are, the tangled mess of them is the same tangled mess as the streets of the city around him, the same tangled mess that is everything else too, the only difference is that this particular mess is his—and maybe there is something to that, but he does not understand how that could be. What does it matter that it was him who walked and crept and climbed all through the city the way that he did, what kind of sense would that make, to have come all this way and done all this work and end up with just that. He wanted so much more and now here he is with just himself and how excited he was, and all the haphazard, erratic lines of his many, many forays out into the city's streets and he stops at that, even though he is so close to something, he may not realize it yet but he is, it has been there all along and he just has to notice it under everything else that he wishes it would have been. It will come, he just needs time, to work through everything else to get there, and that is enough of it for one morning. He stands up and he puts his shoes on, he does not bother trying to untangle his hair, he just ties it up and he leaves, he goes down to the kitchens to get something to eat. He does not stay, he gets a cup of coffee and a sandwich and he goes back up to his studio. He would have gone past the library, before, and now he loops around it, to be sure he does not accidentally come across Amalia either coming or going; he goes up a flight of stairs and comes out into a corridor and here is Amalia anyway. Luca sees her and she looks tired, and sad, and her step is not as light as he remembers and no, he does not want to remember, his stomach clenches and he is not going to say anything, he is going to walk past her but Amalia says, Luca, I leave in three days, and Luca stops, and it does not matter so much anymore that he is angry, that he is hurt, that anything that happened had happened like it did. He stops, and Amalia says, please can we say goodbye.

They stand facing one another and they do not know what to do, they are not sure how to reach around the hurt between them, and maybe it is Luca who takes a half step forward or maybe it is Amalia and it does not matter. They have come close together and they hug, they hold one another for the last time, and then they step away. There are tears in their eyes and they are both smiling slightly, and Amalia says, goodbye Luca, and Luca says, goodbye Amalia. And that is all.

Acknowledgements

First, I want to thank Dartington College of Arts for the time I spent there, and all my tutors, professors, and friends who made the experience as profoundly transformative as it was. What I learned there was foundational to the way that I now write. I would especially like to thank Olchar Lindsann, Uta Baldauf, Bryony Henderson, and Michelle Horacek for helping to keep the spirit of the place present in my life in all the years since.

I am grateful to have had the help of good friends while working on this book. I would like to thank Jamie Woollard, Nisa Malli, and Leigh Gillam for their care, support, and criticism. This would have been a lesser book if not for you.

I would also like to thank Dean Garlick, Klara du Plessis, and Razielle Aigen for the chance to read their work as it took shape and to share my own, and most of all for the warmth and generosity that have always marked the times that we meet.

Emma Hooper, thank you for your friendship for all these years and your kind words. And also thank you for talking me into applying to Dartington in the first place.

Two years ago, I lost a very good friend: Barry Corber (1951-2018). I am grateful that he had the chance to read the manuscript and share with me his thoughts on it before he passed.

I am immensely proud that this book was published by Pedlar Press. Thank you to Beth Follett, for all the work you have done over these many years, and thank you to Monica Kidd for stepping up to keep that work going. It has been a pleasure working with you.

And I would like to say thanks to everyone working behind the scenes to make this book possible. Thank you Emma Allain for your amazing design work, Ken Sparling for your close eye in copy-editing, and everyone working the presses at Coach House Printing.

Thank you to Ben Sack for the perfect drawing on the cover of the book. Ever since I first found your work I have had trouble imagining this book looking any other way. And thank you to Mathieu Gagnon for the picture of me in the back.

And, finally, I would like to thank Megann Ayotte. This book was hard to write, and was a very, very long time in coming. I was not always sure that I had it in me to make it to the end. Thank you, Megann, for being there with me, for nudging me when I needed it, and for helping me to see this book through. I love you so much.

Alan Reed is the author of two previous books: *Isobel & Emile*, a novel, and *For Love of the City*, a collection of poems. Originally from Edmonton, he left to study semiotics at the University of Toronto and then writing at Dartington College of Arts. He now lives in Montreal.